THE
Enid Blyton
BEDTIME
STORY BOOK

THE Enid Blyton BEDTIME STORY BOOK

Illustrated by
Maureen Bradley Lynn N. Grundy
Sally Holmes and Ken Stott

TREASURE PRESS

First published in Great Britain in 1980 by
Hodder & Stoughton Ltd under the title
The Enid Blyton Goodnight Story Book

This edition published in 1988 by
Treasure Press
59 Grosvenor Street
London W1

ISBN 1 85051 266 3

Printed in Hong Kong

Contents

The Old Black Horse

There was once an old black horse who
lived by himself in Long Meadow. He was
past work and he spent his days pulling at
the juicy grass, and remembering his old
friends and the good times they had had
together.

He was lonely. His friends were far
away, still at work for one farmer or
another. There were sheep in the next field,
but the old horse thought them stupid
creatures. There were rabbits in his own
field, but they always ran off as soon as
they heard his heavy hoofs.

'I wouldn't mind a dog to talk to sometimes,' thought the old horse. 'I've known
some friendly dogs in my time – clever
dogs too. But the farmer's two dogs are
surly creatures, and never come near me.'

At the cottage down the road lived a
boy. He was big for his age, and stronger
than the other lads. The old horse sometimes saw him passing by the gate, but he
always kept out of the way. He didn't want
to make friends with that boy!

Tom didn't make friends with anything or anyone! He had quickly found out that he was bigger and stronger than most children of his age, and so he had always got his own way by pushing the others down, or hitting them hard. The other boys and girls were afraid of him, and Tom soon knew that. He liked them to be afraid of him. He liked them to run away when he came along. It made him feel grand and strong and important. He wasn't nice to animals either. He wanted them to be afraid of him too!

And they were. The old horse galloped off to the other end of the field when Tom came by. He knew quite well that Tom could throw stones very hard. It was better to be out of the boy's way! All the cats and dogs ran off when Tom came by, too. He could pull a cat's tail hard, and twist a dog's collar till the poor creature almost choked.

One day the old horse saw, to his great surprise, that Tom had a dog of his own! It was a big, clumsy puppy, with wide brown eyes and a tail that wagged gaily. Someone had given it to the boy, and Tom meant to make it the most obedient dog in the world.

'I've no use for animals who won't do what they are told!' he said to the other boys. 'My dog is going to be my slave. When I say "Come" it will come, and when I say "Go" it will go. When I say "Lie down" it will lie down at once.'

That was exactly like Tom. He wasn't going to make a loving friend of his dog – he was going to make it a poor frightened little slave. And he began at once.

The puppy was put on a short lead. He was made to walk close by Tom's legs, almost choking. He was hit when he did

8

not understand an order from Tom. He was scolded the whole time, and never praised or loved.

He soon lost the wag out of his tail, and his ears drooped. He began to be afraid of Tom. He was a dear playful puppy, but as soon as Tom came near he crouched down on the ground and put his tail between his legs.

Tom used to give the puppy his lessons in the lane by the field where the old horse lived. The horse watched through a gap in the hedge. He liked dogs, and he thought the puppy looked a jolly fellow. He felt very sorry for him.

The puppy soon learnt to do what he was told, because he knew that if he didn't he would be struck hard with a stick, or have his collar pulled at so hard that it hurt him. He was taught all sorts of things, but he did them out of fear, not out of love.

One day Tom took the puppy down the lane. He met Harry, Len and Mollie. 'Hallo,' he said. 'See my pup? Like to

watch him do some tricks?'

The other children stood and watched. The puppy was told what he was to do. 'Now I'm going to throw my stick into this pond, and you are to fetch it,' said Tom.

The puppy listened. He looked at the pond. There were ducks on it and he didn't like ducks. They flapped big wings at him. Splash! Tom's stick went into the pond, and he shouted to the puppy.

'Fetch it! Fetch it!'

But the puppy wouldn't. He crouched down on the ground and shivered. The other children laughed. Tom was very angry.

'What! You won't obey me, you tiresome little thing!' he yelled. 'You shall have a beating.'

He struck the puppy with a stick and the dog howled in pain.

'Don't,' said Mollie. 'You're cruel.'

'Stop,' said Harry. 'He's only a pup.'

'I'll beat you too, if you give me orders about my own dog!' said Tom, angrily.

9

The puppy howled again.

The old horse had been watching. He was afraid of Tom, too – but he couldn't bear to hear the dog whining so pitifully. He suddenly jumped over the hedge, and landed near the children with a crash. They all jumped, and the puppy fled behind a bush in fear.

The horse cantered up to Tom. He put his big head behind the boy's back and caught hold of his belt with his teeth. Tom felt himself suddenly jerked off his feet. Holding him tightly, though the boy was struggling hard, the old horse trotted a little way down the lane to where a big holly bush stood. The horse knew how prickly it was, for he had pricked his nose on it many times. With a jerk of his strong head he threw the boy straight into the middle of the bush!

'Ow-yow-ow!' yelled Tom, as the prickles stuck into him. 'Ow-yow-ow! You horrid thing! Get me out, Harry, quick!'

But Harry didn't. He stood and laughed. So did the others. 'It serves you right,' said Harry. 'I'm not a bit sorry for you, Tom. You are always using your strength to hurt others weaker or smaller than yourself – and now someone stronger than you is using his strength to punish *you*. Ha, ha!'

Tom wriggled out of the bush, yelling with pain and anger. He fell to the ground, jumped up, and rushed at Harry to hit him. But the old horse stepped in again, caught hold of Tom, and this time swung him right over and into the duck-pond.

There was a frightened scurrying of ducks – and splash! Tom was in the muddy water. He came up gasping and spluttering, to see the other children screaming with laughter.

'Good old horse! It serves you right, Tom!'

The farmer came up, grinning, as Tom waded out of the pond, wet and muddy. He laid his hand on the old horse's neck.

'The old horse has done what I've longed to do many a time, my lad!' he said. 'Let it be a lesson to you. You're a bully – and my old horse has bullied you, so that you know now what it's like. Not very pleasant, is it? I've watched you bullying that pup of yours – and the other children, too. You go home and get dry – and make up your mind in the future that you will be a friend to others, and not an enemy.'

Tom went off, crying. The children ran home. The farmer put the horse back into the field, giving him a pat on his long nose. The puppy squeezed through a gap in the hedge and ran to the old horse's shaggy feet.

'Thank you,' he wuffed. 'You saved me from a beating. Perhaps Tom will be nicer now.'

'Maybe,' neighed the old horse. 'And maybe not. But you just come and tell me when he's not, and I'll deal with him again. We'll be friends, you and I.'

'We will!' yelped the puppy in delight, and galloped round and about the old horse. 'Come on – let's have a race. I like you. You're the nicest horse I've ever met.'

And now the two are great friends, and the old horse isn't lonely any more. Tom knows quite well that his puppy tells the old horse everything, and he is very careful to be kind to him instead of cruel. He doesn't want to be thrown into the pond again! It was a good thing for everyone that the old black horse was sensible enough that summer's day to put matters right himself, wasn't it?

The Greedy Rabbit

'Let's have a picnic!' cried Loppy, frisking round his mother. 'Do, do, do! There is lettuce to eat, carrots to nibble and turnips too! Mother, let's have a picnic!'

'Very well,' said his mother. 'Go and tell the others, and we'll have a picnic this very afternoon. Ask your friends in the burrow next door too, if you like.'

Loppy bounded off, very happy. He told all his brothers and sisters about the picnic and then they went to ask their friends.

'We'll ask Furry, because she's so sweet and gentle,' said Loppy. 'And Whiskers because he's such fun. And Bobtail because he knows how to play so many games.'

'And Fluff because he's the baby,' said the others. 'But *not* Slippy, because he's so sly and greedy,' said Loppy. 'I don't like him.'

'Neither do we!' cried everyone. So Furry, Whiskers, Bobtail and Fluff were asked – but not Slippy!

Slippy was angry. He watched them all setting off to the picnic, carrying baskets and bags, chattering away happily. He frowned and pulled at his whiskers.

'Nasty things!' he said. 'Horrid mean things! I'd like to spoil their picnic and eat all the things myself! That would just punish them for their meanness to me!'

He sat and thought for a little while – and then an idea came into his sly little head.

'I know! I know! I'll creep under a bush just behind them, when they are having the picnic – and I'll shout out: 'Fox! Fox!' Then they'll all rush off to their holes – and I shall be able to sit down and eat everything by myself. Ho, ho, what a fine trick!'

The sly little rabbit set off after the others. He waited until they were all sitting in a ring, munching carrots, lettuces and turnips, and then he went down a hole, and came up again beneath a bush nearby.

'FOX! FOX!' he yelled. 'FOX! Beware! He is coming. FOX!'

'Oooh. Eeee! Oooh!' squealed the frightened rabbits, and they rushed off down the hill at once, popping into the first holes they saw. The feast was left on the grass – and it wasn't long before Slippy crept out from under the bush and sat down to finish the tit-bits!

He was sitting there very happily indeed, when a sound made him jump. It was the crack of a twig just behind him!

He looked round, his big ears twitching and his nose going up and down in fright.

Tails and whiskers, it was a FOX! Yes – but a *real* one this time! A great red fox with a fine bushy tail sticking out behind him! His sharp nose sniffed Slippy, and he grinned.

'A rabbit!' he said. 'A nice, fat little rabbit – all by himself, and having a grand feast! Ho! What a nice dinner he will make!'

He pounced – but Slippy was off in a trice, shouting: 'Help! Help!'

But nobody helped him. Everyone had been so frightened when he had called out 'Fox!' before, that now they were all hiding at the bottom of their holes, and not a single rabbit was around to tell him how to escape.

Slippy ran down the hill, and the fox ran after him. Slippy ran under a bush. The fox followed. Slippy tried to get to a hole, but the fox wouldn't let him go near it. Slippy turned and twisted, dodged and dived – but he could *not* get near a hole and go down it. His little heart thumped hard, and he felt sure that he would soon be so tired that he would have to lie down – and then the fox would snap him up!

'Why did I play that mean trick!' he thought. 'Oh, what a punishment this is! Help, help!'

And then a big pheasant, who hated the fox because he had taken her young ones, saw the hunted rabbit. The bird flew to a nearby bush and cried: 'Here come the dogs! Here come the dogs!'

Now the fox was as frightened of the dogs as the rabbits were of the fox – and off he ran at once, his bushy tail streaming out behind him! Slippy sank down, trembling. In a few moments rabbits popped up their heads, and the pheasant told them all that had happened.

'It was my fault!' said Slippy. 'I spoilt the picnic by calling "Fox!" so that I might eat the tit-bits – and when you had all gone, and I was feasting, a fox *really* came – and nearly caught me. It served me right. I'll never, never be greedy or mean again!'

And as he is always asked to every picnic now, I think he must have kept is word!

Pink Paint for a Pixie

Once, when Linda was playing at the bottom of her garden, she heard a funny noise. She stopped and listened.

'If a bird could speak, it would speak just like that funny voice,' thought Linda, in surprise. 'It *is* somebody talking – it's a very small voice, high and clear.'

She sat perfectly still, listening, trying to hear what the voice said.

'Just my luck!' said the voice. 'Finished the tea-set all but three cups – and now I've run out of paint. Isn't that just my luck?'

Linda quietly popped her head through a gap in the hedge to see who could be talking. It didn't at all sound like a child. It wasn't a child, either.

'It's a pixie!' said Linda, in the greatest surprise. 'Well, who would have thought I'd ever see a pixie! I've looked for years and years and never seen one. But this *must* be one – and he's talking to himself. What is he doing?'

She looked closely and saw that he was painting a very small tea-set, just big enough for himself to drink from. The cups and saucers were about the size of the ones in Linda's doll's house.

Suddenly the tiny fellow heard Linda breathing and he looked up. He stared in surprise at the little girl's head peeping through the hedge.

'Hullo!' he said. 'Isn't it a nuisance – I've run out of pink paint.'

'What are you doing?' asked Linda.

'I'm painting a pretty picture on these

cups,' said the pixie, and he held one up for Linda to see.

He certainly was putting a very pretty pattern on each one. There were pink roses, and green leaves all the way round. The saucers and plates had the same pattern.

Linda looked at the tiny tubes of paint beside the pixie. The tube of pink paint was squeezed quite empty.

'Can't you finish your work?' she asked.

'No,' said the pixie. 'And I promised the Princess Peronel she should have the whole set tomorrow, for her birthday party. It's really annoying.'

Linda suddenly had a splendid idea. *She* had some tubes of paint in her paint-box. One might be pink. If so, she could lend it to the pixie!

'I believe I could help you,' she said. 'I've got some paints. I'll go and get the tube of pink. Wait here a minute.'

She ran indoors and found her paint-box. 'Darling, surely you are not going to paint indoors this fine morning!' said her mother, when she saw Linda getting out her paint-box.

'No, Mummy – I'm lending a tube of pink paint to a pixie,' said Linda.

Her mother laughed. 'What funny things you do say, Linda!' she said. She didn't guess for a minute that Linda was speaking the truth. She thought she was just pretending.

Linda ran out again, holding in her hand a tube of crimson paint. She knew that if the pixie mixed the deep red with water, the colour would be pink. She was soon back at the hedge again.

'Here you are,' she said. 'I'm sure this will make a lovely pink.'

'You *are* a good friend!' said the pixie, gratefully. 'You can watch me paint if you like.'

Linda sat and watched him. He had a tiny china palette on which he mixed his colours. He squeezed some of the crimson out on to it, and then dipped his tiny brush into a dewdrop hanging on a grass nearby. Soon he had just the right pink for the little cups. It was fun to watch him painting roses round the cup he was holding.

'I don't know what I should have done if you hadn't helped me,' he said. 'Can I do anything for you in return?'

'I suppose you couldn't make a wish come true, could you?' asked Linda, at once. The pixie shook his head.

'No,' he said. 'I don't know powerful enough magic for that. If I did I'd have wished for a new tube of pink paint for myself. But if you really want a wish to come true why don't you find a four-leaved clover, put it under your pillow, and wish before you go to sleep?'

'There aren't any four-leaved clovers round about here,' said Linda. 'I and the other children have looked and looked, but we have never found one.'

'Well, go to where the foxgloves grow, pick up a fallen foxglove bell, slip it on your thumb and wish,' said the pixie.

'The foxgloves aren't out yet,' said Linda.

'Of course they aren't!' said the pixie. 'How silly of me. Well, try the pink-tipped daisy spell, then.'

'What's that?' asked Linda.

'You pick thirteen pink-tipped daisies,' said the pixie. 'You make them into a daisy-chain, and wear them round your neck for one hour, at four o'clock in the daytime. You wish your wish thirteen times in that hour. Then you take off the chain and put the daisies in water. You mustn't forget to do that, because if you don't give them a drink, the magic won't work.'

'That sounds a good spell,' said Linda. 'But there aren't any pink-tipped daisies round here, Pixie. Look – they are quite white.'

The little girl picked two or three daisies and showed them to the pixie. He looked underneath the petals at the very tips. He shook his head.

'You're right,' he said. 'Not a pink tip to

be seen. Very tiresome. Well, I must think of something else for you.'

A bell rang in the distance. Linda got up. 'That's for my dinner,' she said. 'I must go. I'll come back again afterwards.'

'I'll think of something whilst you are gone,' said the pixie. He thought and he thought. But he could think of no other way of making a wish come true. He was only a small pixie, not very old, and he really didn't know a great deal of magic.

Then a fine idea came into his small head. Hadn't he got plenty of pink paint in that tube? Well, why shouldn't he paint all the daisies round about with pink tips?

'Good idea!' he said, and as soon as he finished his tea-set, he went to the daisies, sat underneath the little flowers, and carefully ran his brush, full of pink paint, under the tip of each petal. Soon the first daisy looked really pretty. It turned up its

petals a little to show the pink underneath.

'I hope Linda comes back soon,' thought the pixie. 'Then I can tell her what I've done.'

But Linda didn't come back. Her mother had said she must have a rest after dinner, and the little girl was on her bed, hoping that the pixie would still be in the field when she got up at three o'clock.

He wasn't. He had packed up his painted tea-set for the Princess Peronel and had gone. But there were the daisies, all pink-tipped! And there was the little tube of paint left beside them, half-empty now, with the top put neatly on.

Linda looked round for the pixie, when she crept out through the hedge into the field after her rest. He wasn't there. But there was her tube of paint – and, oh, what a surprise, it was lying by a daisy-plant, where four pink-tipped daisies grew together, their golden eyes looking straight at Linda!

'He's painted your tips pink! The underneath of your pretty white petals in crimson pink! Now I can try that magic spell!'

Linda picked thirteen daisies and made them into a chain. You know how she made it, don't you? She slit each stalk near its end with a pin, and then slipped a daisy through the slit, so that soon the thirteen were hanging in a pretty chain. She joined the chain – and looked at her watch.

'Four o'clock. Now I'll wear it – and for one hour I will wish my wish thirteen times!'

She wore the daisy-chain, and wished her wish thirteen times in the hour. Then she took off the chain and put the daisies into water to have a drink. She wished for her big soldier-brother to come back from far away – and, will you believe it, he came home the very next day. She rushed out to tell the pixie, but she has never seen him again.

Have you seen pink-tipped daisies? Go out and look for some; maybe you will find thirteen!

The Man Who Wasn't Father Christmas

There was once an old man with a long white beard who loved children. He was very poor, so he couldn't give the children anything, and you can guess that he always wished at Christmas-time that he was Father Christmas.

'Goodness! What fun I'd have if I were Father Christmas!' he thought. 'Think of having a sack that was always full of toys – that couldn't be emptied, because it was magic. How happy I should be!'

Now one Christmas-time the old man saw a little notice in the window of a big shop. This is what it said:

'WANTED. A man with a white beard to be Father Christmas, and give out paper leaflets in the street.'

Well, the old man stared at this notice, and wondered if he could get the job. How lovely to dress up as Father Christmas, and go up and down the streets with all the children staring at him! He would be so happy.

So he marched into the shop and asked if he could have the job.

'The work is not hard,' said the shop-man. 'All you have to do is to dress up in a red cloak and trousers and big boots, and take a sack with you.'

'Will it be full of toys?' asked the old man, his eyes shining at the thought.

'Of course not!' said the shopman. 'It will be full of leaflets for you to give to the passers-by. I have had these leaflets printed to tell everyone to come to our shop this Christmas and buy their presents here. I thought it would be a good idea to dress somebody up as Father Christmas, and let him give out the leaflets.'

'I see,' said the old man. 'I rather thought it would be nice to give the children something.'

'Well, what an idea!' said the shopman. 'Now, see if this red Father Christmas costume fits you.'

It fitted the old man well. He got into it and looked at himself in the glass. He really looked exactly like old Father Christmas. His long white beard flowed down over his chest and his bright blue eyes twinkled brightly.

He took his sack of leaflets and went out. It was the day before Christmas and everyone was busy shopping. How the children stared when they saw the old man walking along in the road!

'It's Father Christmas!' they shouted. 'It's Father Christmas! Come and see him!'

Soon the children were crowding round the old man, asking if they could peep into his sack. But alas, there were no toys there, and all he had to give the children were the leaflets. The children were disappointed.

'Fancy Father Christmas only giving us leaflets about Mr White's shop,' they said. 'We thought he was a kind old man – but he isn't. He didn't even give us a sweet.'

The old man heard the children saying these things and he was sad. 'I made a mistake in taking this job,' he said to himself. 'It is horrid to pretend to be somebody kind and not be able to give the boys and girls even a penny! I feel dreadful!'

It began to snow. The old man plodded along the streets, giving out his leaflets. And suddenly he heard a curious sound. It was the sound of bells!

'Where are those bells, I wonder?' thought the old man, looking all round. 'It sounds like horse-bells. But everyone has cars nowadays. There are no horses in this town.'

It wasn't horse-bells he heard. It was reindeer-bells! To the great surprise of the old man, a large sleigh drove down the road, drawn by reindeer. And in it was –

well, you can guess without being told – the *real* Father Christmas!

The sleigh drew up, and Father Christmas leaned out. 'Am I anywhere near the town of Up-and-Down?' he called. Then he stared hard at the old man – and he frowned.

'You look like *me*!' he said. 'Why are you dressed like that?'

'Well, just to get a job of work,' said the old man. 'But really because I love children, and I thought if I dressed up like you, they would think I *was* you, and would come round me and be happy. But all I have in my sack is stupid leaflets about somebody's shop – I haven't any toys to give away, as you have. So instead of making the children happy I have disappointed them. I am sorry now I ever took this job.'

'Well, well, you did it for the best,' said Father Christmas, smiling suddenly. 'I like people who love children. They are always the nicest people, you know. Look here –

would you like to do me a good turn?'

'I'd love to,' said the old man.

'Well,' said Father Christmas, 'I haven't had any tea, and I feel so hungry and thirsty. Would you mind taking care of my reindeer for me whilst I'm in a tea-shop? They don't like standing still, so you'll have to drive them round and round the town. And if you meet any children, you must do exactly as I always do.'

'What's that?' asked the old man, his eyes shining.

'You must stop, and say to them, "A happy Christmas to you! What would you like out of my sack?" And you must let the child dip its hand into my sack and take out what it wants. You won't mind doing that, will you? I always do that as I drive along.'

'*Mind* doing that! It would be the thing I would like best in the world,' said the old man, hardly believing his ears. 'It's – it's – it's – well, I just can't tell you how happy it will make me. I can't believe it's true!'

Father Christmas smiled his wide smile. He jumped down from the sleigh and threw the reins to the old man.

'Come back in an hour,' he said. 'I'll have finished my tea by then.'

He went into a tea-shop. The old man climbed into the driving-seat. He was trembling with joy. He looked at the enormous sack beside him on the seat. It was simply bursting with toys! He cracked the whip and the reindeer set off with a jingling of bells.

Soon they met three children. How those children stared! Then they went quite mad with delight and yelled to the old man: 'Father Christmas! Father Christmas! Stop a minute, do!'

The old man stopped the reindeer. He beamed at the children. 'A happy Christmas to you!' he said. 'What would you like out of my sack?'

'An engine, please,' said the boy.

'A doll, please,' said one of the girls.

'A book, please,' said another girl.

in a happy dream, took off his red clothes and went home.

'I've never been so happy before,' he said as he got into bed. 'Never! If only people knew how wonderful it is to give happiness to others! How lucky Father Christmas is to go about the world giving presents to all the boys and girls!'

The old man hung up his stocking, though he felt rather ashamed of it. And when he woke up in the morning, what do you think was in it?

A magic purse was in it – a purse that was always full of pennies! No matter how many were taken out, there were always some left.

'A penny-purse – a magic penny-purse!' cried the old man joyfully. 'My word – what fun I'll have with the children now!'

He does – for he always has a penny to give each one. I wonder if you've ever seen the little penny-purse. It is black and has two letters in silver on the front. They are 'F.C.' I expect you can guess what they stand for!

'Dip into my sack and find what you want,' said the old man. And with shining faces the three children dipped in their hands . . . and each of them pulled out exactly what he wanted! They rushed home with shouts of joy.

Well, the old man stopped at every child he met, wished them a happy Christmas, and asked them what they wanted. And dozens of happy children dipped into the enormous sack and pulled out just what they longed for.

At the end of an hour the old man drove the reindeer back to the tea-shop. Father Christmas was waiting, putting on his big fur gloves. He smiled when he saw the bright face of the old man.

'You've had a good time, I can see,' he said. 'Thanks so much. I don't give presents to grown-ups usually – but you might hang up your stocking just for fun tonight. Goodbye!'

He drove off with a ringing of sleigh-bells. The old man went back to the shop

Annabelle's Little Thimble

Annabelle had a nice little workbasket that Granny had given her. You should have seen it! There were needles of all sizes, a bright pair of scissors, black, white, grey, green and blue cottons, and a pincushion. But best and brightest of all was Annabelle's little silver thimble.

Mummy had given that to her on her birthday. It was made of real silver, so it shone and glittered brightly. It fitted Annabelle's middle finger beautifully, and she was very proud of it.

She took great care to keep her workbasket shut when Rascal the Jackdaw was about. He was a tame jackdaw that Daddy had picked up from the ground when he was a tiny bird, fallen from the nest. Daddy had fed him and tamed him and now he hopped and flew around the house, and loved to talk to anyone he met.

But he was so fond of bright things that everyone was careful not to leave any spoons, brooches, necklaces or silver pencils about. If they did Rascal the Jackdaw would take them and hide them away in one of his cubby-holes in the garden. Once Daddy had found a whole collection of things tucked away in a corner of the potting-shed – a pair of scissors, two spoons from next door, some pieces of silver paper and a little gilt pin!

Rascal couldn't help taking them because he was so fond of shiny things. Daddy had often smacked him on the beak for going off with things, but it didn't cure him! So everyone had to be very careful not to leave glittering things about.

Annabelle had always been careful of her little thimble, because she had seen Rascal looking at it two or three times, when she put it on her finger. But there came a morning when she forgot.

She was sewing a new bonnet for her doll when Mummy called her. 'Quick, Annabelle! There's Auntie Sue!'

Annabelle loved Auntie Sue so she hurriedly put down her work, stuck her thimble on top of it and ran to meet her Auntie.

And as soon as she was safely out of the door Rascal the Jackdaw came in at the window! He spied the bright little thimble at once and pounced on it. Ah! He had wanted that for ever so long. Where should he put it?

He went and sat on the kitchen window-sill, holding it in his beak. Cook was busy making Christmas puddings, and she didn't even look at him. Rascal watched her. Dear me, cook had lots of bright things too, on the table beside her!

Yes – she had six five pence pieces, four two pence pieces, a silver elephant, very small, a tiny silver doll, a little silver horseshoe and one big, bright ten pence piece. She was going to put them in the Christmas pudding for luck! It was always fun at Christmas time to see who got the treasures out of the pudding.

Rascal watched cook drop the shining things into the pudding. He thought cook was hiding them. What a good place to hide them! He waited until Cook went to the cupboard to get something and then he hopped to the table. He dropped Annabelle's silver thimble into the sticky mixture and then covered it neatly up with the currants and chopped nuts in the dish. Ha! It was a splendid hiding-place!

But oh dear me, what a to-do when Annabelle ran to get her sewing again! Where was her dear little silver thimble? Gone! Nowhere to be found at all! Everyone hunted all over the place, but it couldn't be found.

'Rascal must have taken it,' said poor Annabelle in tears. So Daddy went to look in all the hidey-holes he knew the jackdaw had. But they were empty. Not one of them had poor Annabelle's thimble in it.

Annabelle was very unhappy. She did so like her thimble, and besides Mummy had given it to her. It was dreadful to lose something Mummy had bought for her. No other thimble would be half so nice!

'Perhaps someone will give you another one at Christmas time,' said Mummy, kissing her.

'It won't be as nice as the one *you* gave me, Mummy!' said Annabelle. 'It helped me to sew so nicely. I shan't sew so well with any other thimble, I'm sure!'

'Rubbish!' said Mummy, smiling. She made up her mind to ask Annabelle's Auntie Sue to give the little girl another thimble for Christmas. Mummy wanted to give Annabelle a new doll. Auntie Sue promised Mummy she would buy a lovely new thimble for Annabelle.

But, you know, she forgot about it! Yes, she bought Annabelle a fairy-tale book instead – so when Christmas morning came there was no silver thimble for Annabelle! She was so disappointed. But she didn't say anything, of course. She loved all her presents very much, especially her new doll – but she *would* have liked a new thimble!

Christmas dinner-time came. What a big turkey there was – and what a lot of people to eat it! Granny and Grandpa, three aunties, two uncles and Cousin Jan and Cousin Jimmy, as well as Annabelle herself and Mummy and Daddy. But there was quite enough for everybody!

Then Cook brought in the Christmas pudding with a bit of holly stuck on top. How the children clapped their hands! What a splendid pudding it looked!

'Hope I get two pence!' cried Cousin Jane.

'Hope I get five pence!' cried Cousin Jimmy.

'And I hope I get the little silver elephant!' cried Annabelle. Everyone was served, and then what a hunt there was

through the pieces of pudding to see if anyone had been lucky.

'Two pence for me!' cried Daddy. 'Hurrah!'

'Five pence for me!' cried Cousin Jimmy fishing out a coin from his piece of pudding.

'What have *I* got?' cried Annabelle, feeling her spoon scrape against something hard. She looked at the treasure *she* had – and then she cried out in astonishment.

'Mummy! Daddy! It's my own little silver thimble that I lost ages ago! Oh, look, How did it come in the pudding? Oh, it's my own dear little thimble!'

Mummy and Daddy *were* surprised! Annabelle ran out to ask Cook if she knew it had been put into the pudding, but Cook didn't know anything about it at all!

'I expect it's a little trick Santa Claus played on you!' she said.

'Caw, caw, caw!' suddenly said a loud voice, and Rascal the jackdaw looked in at the window.

'Oh, Rascal, I wonder if *you* took my thimble and dropped it into the pudding!' cried Annabelle. 'Did you, Rascal?'

'Caw, caw, caw!' said the jackdaw. And Annabelle didn't know whether he meant yes or no! But she didn't mind; she had got back her little silver thimble after all. It was the nicest Christmas surprise she had had!

The Shepherd Boy and the Goblin

There was once a shepherd boy who lived out on the hills, watching his sheep. With him was his dog, Lassie, a wise and loving animal, ready to do anything in the world for her little master.

There were goblins on the hillside. Dick, the shepherd boy, had often seen them, and had kept well out of their way, for he knew them to be ill-natured creatures, and ready to catch him and make him their servant if they only could!

One night, Dick saw a goblin coming along quietly with an empty sack over his back. He did not see the shepherd boy, who was behind a bush with his dog.

Lassie was about to growl, but Dick laid his hand on her and she lay silent.

Dick peered round the bush in the moonlight. To his enormous surprise he saw the goblin go to a stone that lay close to the hillside and twist it round. An entrance to a cave showed up, big and black.

'So that's where the goblins go to get their treasure!' thought Dick. 'Oho! I may pay that cave a visit myself, if I have a chance!'

He watched till the goblin came out again, this time with a *full* sack on his shoulder. The little creature staggered down the hill, muttering to himself, and as he went something rolled out of the sack.

When the goblin had gone, Dick picked up what had rolled from the sack. It was a gleaming diamond! The boy whistled in surprise. Riches in the hill! Riches to make his mother and father, and all his sisters and brothers happy, well-fed and well-shod! Aha! He would take a sack himself and go to fill it that very morning.

He called his father to look after the sheep, and whistled to his dog, Lassie, to come with him. Then, a sack over his shoulder, and his dog by his side, the boy went to the big stone in the hillside.

He twisted it as he had seen the goblin

do. It swung round – and there lay the black, cold cave! Dick stepped inside, and the dog came too. He went in for a good way – and then stopped in wonder! All round the cave-wall glistened brilliant stones, some green, some red, some white, some blue!

'I shall be richer than any man in the world!' thought the boy. He began to fill his sack full. In went the precious stones, one on top of another till the sack was almost too heavy to lift. When it would hold not one more stone Dick began to lift it on to his shoulder.

And then a harsh voice spoke in the darkness of the cave.

'You have filled your sack well, shepherd boy! Can you not get one more thing into it?'

A lantern shone, and a goblin crept out of the darkness. Then came another goblin – and another – and another. The boy was surrounded, and his heart beat fast as he saw so many of the ugly little creatures coming near to him.

Lassie growled, but Dick stopped her. He was afraid that the goblins might turn her into a rock or a clod of earth if she offended them.

'Ho!' said the first goblin, peering into the sack. 'A good haul! How dare you come and rob us of our jewels!'

'They are not yours,' said Dick. 'They belong to anyone who finds them. This hill does not belong to you!'

'Oh, yes, it does!' said the goblin. 'It has been ours for nine-hundred years! See, brothers! See how many of our precious stones he meant to steal!'

'It is a wonder he could lift the sack!' said another, angrily.

'He could not get one more stone in!' said a third. 'It is full to the brim! Anything else would roll out!'

'How shall we punish him?' asked the first goblin.

'He shall serve us for one-hundred years and a day!' shouted all the goblins.

'That I will not!' said Dick stoutly. 'You have no right to keep me here. I will not take your jewels, if you think them yours. I will leave them here in the sack. Now let me go, or it will be the worse for you.'

'And who do you think will find you here?' said the first goblin, mockingly. 'No one knows this cave save ourselves. No, my boy – you shall be our servant. You shall fetch and carry, cook and sweep. How you will long to see the sun – for never again will you step outside this hill!'

'Do not keep me here,' said Dick. 'Let me go. I must see to my sheep. I am sorry I took your jewels. I will keep the secret of your cave to myself. No one shall ever know it.'

'Shall we let him go, brothers?' said the first goblin, with a wicked grin.

'Yes – on one condition!' shouted another goblin. 'If he – or his dog – can put another thing into that full sack, we will let them go!'

'Ho, ho!' roared the goblins, knowing quite well that the sack was already full to the brim. 'Yes! Now, boy, try!' But try as he would, Dick could not get anything else into that sack! Stones rolled out – earth would not stay – nothing else could be put there, for the sack was already quite full.

The dog was lying watching, her big brown eyes wise and thoughtful. When her master had finished trying, and was sitting in despair on the cave floor, the dog stood up and went to the sack.

'And now the dog is going to try!' shouted the mischievous goblins, enjoying their cruel joke. 'Come, dog – if *you* can put anything more into the sack, you and your master shall go free!'

'Woof!' said Lassie – and she straightway bit a large hole in the sack. Then she turned to Dick, who had sprung to his feet in delight.

'She has put something in the sack that wasn't there before!' he cried. 'She has put a hole in it! See! *Now* what do you say, goblins? Set us free!'

The goblins frowned and grumbled and shook their fists at Lassie – but it was no use, they must keep their word and set the boy and the dog free. Sullenly, they stood aside to let them pass, and the two ran up the dark cave and out into the golden sunshine.

'Lassie, Lassie, you clever dog!' cried Dick, hugging the delighted animal, who licked him again and again. 'You are wiser than I am! What should I have done without you!'

He ran to tell his father his adventure – and suddenly he remembered the diamond he had found the night before. He took it from his pocket and showed it to his father.

'We will sell it,' said the man, overjoyed. 'It will buy us many good things.'

It did – and what do you suppose was the very first thing it bought? A new collar for Lassie with her name on it in gold!

'You deserve it!' cried Dick, as he put it on. And she certainly did.

'And I am afraid of the fire,' said the wax sailor-doll. 'I might melt if I were too near.'

'Here comes the imp,' said the pink cat. 'Oh dear! We never get any peace.'

'I wish I could go out to the pond and swim, or waddle about the wet grass outside and look for worms,' said the yellow duck, with a sigh. 'I hate being chased by that nasty imp. Hallo – where's he gone?'

The imp had shot back into his hole in fright! All the toys stared at one another in

Let's Play Worms

There was once a naughty little imp who made his home in a mouse-hole that led into the nursery. His name was Impetty, and he was the greatest tease the toys had ever known.

He would come springing out of the mouse-hole at night and chase the yellow duck till he lost his quack, pull the pink cat's tail till it came loose, and press the teddy-bear's middle till his growl was almost worn out.

The toys didn't like him at all. But they simply couldn't get rid of him. He didn't mind being teased back. He could run so fast that it wasn't a bit of good chasing him. He hadn't any growl to press in the middle, and he hadn't any key to wind him up – so they couldn't steal his key and make him be quiet that way.

'If only we could find out something he is frightened of,' sighed the long-haired doll.

'He isn't frightened of anything in the world,' said the yellow duck.

'He must be frightened of *some*thing,' said the pink cat. 'I am frightened of dogs.'

'And I am frightened of cats,' said the clockwork mouse.

astonishment. Now whatever in the world could have frightened him? What a funny thing!

'What did we say that could have given him a fright?' said the long-haired doll eagerly. 'Think hard everyone Who was speaking when he came out?'

'I was,' said the yellow duck. 'I just said I wished I could go to the pond and swim.'

'What else did you say?' asked the clockwork mouse. 'You said something else, I'm sure.'

The yellow duck thought hard. 'Yes,' he said. 'I said I wished I could go and waddle in the grass and look for worms.'

'Worms! Worms!' shouted the teddy-bear. 'That's it! That's what the imp is frightened of! Now all we've got to do is to get lots of worms and wave them at him and he'll never come back again.'

'Don't be so silly, bear,' said the pink cat. 'As if *we* could get worms! *I've* never seen any wriggling about the nursery carpet.'

'And we can't possibly get out of the window into the garden, for it's shut,' said the golliwog.

'And even if we could get worms we couldn't be so unkind as to wave them about,' said the long-haired doll, who was very tender-hearted. 'Worms indeed! Quite hopeless.'

The teddy-bear looked glum. He sat down on the brick-box and thought hard – and suddenly a grin came over his jolly little face. 'I know!' he cried. 'I know!'

He ran to where Ann and Jerry kept their paint-boxes. He had seen the two children using them the day before. He opened the lids. Inside the boxes were little tubes out of which the children squeezed the colours they wanted. Teddy had noticed that they came out like worms!

'See!' he shouted, and taking off the top, he squeezed a blue tube hard. Out shot a long blue worm! The toys shrieked – what a surprise – and what fun!

They all rushed up to the paint-boxes. Even the wooden skittles rushed up to get a tube too. They wanted to join in the fun, you may be sure! There was one for every one – except for the big golliwog. But what do you think *he* did? He wasn't going to be left out of the fun! He ran to the basin where the taps were, climbed up to the taps, reached up to the shelf where

Ann's tooth-paste was, in a big tube – and took that down to join the toys! Goodness! What a lot of worms there would be – paint worms and tooth-paste worms too!

Soon the imp came running out from his hole again. The toys held their hands behind them, with the tubes of paint and the tooth-paste tube in them. The imp grinned at them. 'Let's play pinch-me-last!' he said.

'No,' said the teddy-bear, 'let's play WORMS!'

He squeezed his tube – out shot a bright red worm! Everyone squeezed the tubes they held – and out sprang blue worms, green worms, yellow worms, black worms, and brown worms! And as for the Golly's tube of tooth-paste, well, you should have seen the enormous white worm that came out of *that*! It made him squeal in delight!

The imp stared in horror. Worms! And more worms! Gracious, every toy had a worm! They were wagging and wriggling everywhere!

'Ow!' he yelled. 'Ow! Take them away!'

But the toys didn't take them away – no, they rushed at Impetty with their coloured paint worms and he tore off in fright. He jumped up into the basin – slid down the slippery sides – and went down the hole at top speed!

'That's the end of *him*!' said the bear in delight. 'My, what fun that was! Look at my worm, everybody! It's a good wriggler.'

The nursery was full of worms – and the toys made so much noise that Ann and Jerry woke up and came creeping to see what the noise was. The toys leapt into the cupboard and lay quiet – but they left behind the squeezed paint-tubes, the tooth-paste, and the worms – what a mess!

'Just look at that,' said Ann in astonishment. 'Someone's been playing with our paints. I wonder why?'

But they never knew. If you know Ann and Jerry, you can tell them what happened – won't they laugh?

The Cheeky Boy

There was once a little boy who loved to be cheeky. He spoke rudely to his mother and father, and he was cheeky even to his teacher.

He thought it was clever! It made him feel rather grand to say rude things. The other children stared at him when he said, 'Shan't!' or 'Won't', and when he put his tongue out behind his mother's back, he felt quite a hero. The other children laughed at him sometimes, but they thought he was rather horrid, all the same.

He thought it was funny to interrupt the grown-ups when they were talking. He kept pulling his mother's arm, and pretending to want something when she was speaking to her friends. He answered cheekily when they asked him polite questions.

'How are you, Timothy?' they would say. 'Do you like school?'

'No, I hate it,' Timothy would answer, which was not at all true. But he thought it was clever to say cheeky things like that. He would contradict people too, and that made his mother cross.

'It's very warm today,' she would say. And Timothy would answer at once: 'It isn't. It's cold as ice!'

'I wish you wouldn't be so cheeky,' his mother would sigh. 'It's so unpleasant.'

Of course, what he wanted was a good spanking, but nobody gave him that, which was a great pity, because in the end he got a much bigger punishment.

It all happened one night. Timmy woke up suddenly, and heard the clock strike twelve. And at that very same moment he saw what looked like a brownie in his bedroom. It was most astonishing. The boy sat up at once.

'Hallo,' said the brownie. 'I've lost my way, somehow. Is this your bedroom?'

'Oh no, it's the kitchen!' said Timothy, in his usual cheeky manner. 'Who are you?'

'I'm a brownie,' said the little fellow.

'Fibber!' said Timothy. 'There aren't any brownies, or fairies, or elves. I know that. Now you just hop off, funny-face!'

The brownie stared at him sternly. 'Have you no manners, boy?' he asked.

'Plenty,' said Timmy. 'Do you want to buy some?'

'Don't be cheeky,' said the brownie, in disgust.

'Would you rather I was nosey?' said Timothy, in his cheekiest voice.

'My word – you must be Timothy, the cheeky boy!' said the brownie, suddenly. 'I've heard people talk about you, and say what a pity it is you haven't been brought up better! No – I don't want you to be nosey. You can be cheeky. Yes – you can be CHEEKY – CHEEKY – CHEEKY!'

And as he spoke, he vanished in a most peculiar way, just as smoke grows thinner and vanishes. Timmy could just hear his voice saying 'CHEEKY' over and over again, and then it stopped, and there was nobody and nothing there.

'A dream!' thought Timothy. 'A silly dream. But wasn't I smart in it? My word, I do feel sharp when I'm cheeky.'

He fell asleep. When he got up the next morning, he dressed as usual, and then went to the mirror to brush his hair, and get his parting straight.

He stared at himself in surprise. His cheeks were both very swollen and he looked most peculiar.

'Now what's happened to me?' thought Timmy, half-frightened. He went downstairs and his father and mother gazed at him in dismay.

'Timmy! Have you got toothache, dear? You poor boy, you must go to the dentist,' said his mother.

'I don't want to,' said Timothy. 'I haven't got toothache.'

'You *must* go, Timmy,' said his mother.

'Shan't,' said Timmy, rudely. His father was just going to scold him when he saw that Timmy's left cheek was getting almost like a balloon!

'Your face is getting worse, my boy,' he said. 'Mother, you must take him to the dentist at once.'

So Timmy had to go. The dentist was astonished to see how swollen the boy's cheeks were, and he had a look at his teeth at once. He took a very long time and Timmy grew impatient.

'Are you going to be all day?' he said. 'It's Saturday and I want to play with Harry.'

The dentist took no notice of Timothy's rudeness. He spoke to his mother. 'I must take a tooth out at the back,' he said. 'It's the only one that I can see that may be causing this terrible swelling.'

So Timothy had a tooth out, but his cheeks didn't go down. No – they seemed even bigger than ever when he left the dentist. His mother looked at him, very worried.

'I wonder if you've got mumps,' she said. 'You know, sometimes your face swells up very much with that. It may be mumps.'

'Mother, I want to go and play with Harry,' said Timmy. 'You make such a fuss! Look – here's Harry's house. I shall go in and play with him. I won't go to the doctors.'

The cheeky, disobedient boy walked in at Harry's gate and knocked at the door – but as soon as Harry's mother opened it, she cried out in horror to see Timothy's swollen face.

'Go away!' she cried. 'There's something the matter with you. Goodness knows what it is – mumps, perhaps. It may be catching, and I don't want you near Harry. You stay away from school till you are better!'

Timmy's mother heard her. She hurried Timmy away at once to the doctor, and he examined the little boy very carefully.

'Very strange,' he said. 'It *may* be mumps, and it may be because of the tooth the dentist took out. Keep him away from all other children till the swelling goes down.'

'I'm going to a party this afternoon,' said Timmy, at once. 'I don't care what you say!'

The doctor stared at the cheeky little

boy and saw that his cheeks were swelling even more. They looked more like balloons than cheeks! He shook his head.

'You'll do as you're told,' he said. 'I'll make you up some medicine to take, which will, I'm afraid, be very nasty. And I'll give you some lotion to bathe your cheeks with. It will smart, but that can't be helped.'

So there was poor Timmy, put to bed on the day of a party, drinking horrible medicine and having his cheeks bathed with a lotion that smarted like stinging-nettles. He felt very sorry indeed for himself and he cried when he was alone. All that day he lay there, seeing nobody, hearing the children go to the party next door. He took his nasty medicine evey hour, and had his cheeks bathed every two hours. He looked at himself in the glass, and was filled with horror when he saw how ugly he looked.

'Mother, will I always look as ugly as this?' asked poor Timmy.

'You'll look all right as soon as your cheeks go down,' said his mother, looking worried and anxious. 'Now, see if you can go to sleep for a bit.'

But Timmy couldn't. He lay and listened to the shouts of laughter from next door, and he heard the popping of crackers. Then, after two or three hours, he heard the children going home. And suddenly he got a fright!

Someone was looking in at his window! It was Harry! He had been to the party next door, and had suddenly thought he would like to have a word with poor Timmy. He had climbed up the old apple tree outside the boy's bedroom, and there he was, grinning through the window.

'Hallo,' said Timmy, hardly able to speak now because his cheeks were so big.

'Timmy! What's the matter with you!' cried Harry, and the grin faded from his face. 'You look simply terrible, I've never seen anyone so ugly in my life.'

'It's awful,' said Timmy. 'I don't know what happened to make me like this. I'm all cheeks.'

'Well,' said Harry, his grin coming back again, suddenly, 'well – we always knew you were a cheeky boy – and now you certainly are the most CHEEKY person I've ever seen – yes, all cheeks. Perhaps it's because you always were cheeky that you've gone like that!'

A voice called out sternly from below the window. 'Harry! Come down at once. You know you've got your best suit on.'

Harry disappeared suddenly. He didn't dare to be cheeky to *his* mother. He respected her too much. Timmy was left alone, thinking hard.

He remembered the funny dream he had had the night before – when he thought he had seen a brownie. Perhaps it *wasn't* a dream! Perhaps it had been real. Perhaps – perhaps – that little fellow had put a sort of spell on him. Timmy remembered his voice saying: 'You can be CHEEKY – CHEEKY – CHEEKY!'

'He'll come again tonight to see what has happened,' thought Timothy. 'I'll ask him to make me right again. I can't go on like this – everyone thinking I'm ill, and not coming near me.'

But the brownie didn't come! Timothy never saw him again. So the next day his cheeks were still swollen and he still had to take the medicine and have his face bathed.

He had a lot of time to think. He began to notice that every time he was rude or cheeky, his cheeks swelled up a little more – but if he answered politely and kindly, they seemed to go down.

'I suppose that the only person who can cure me is myself,' thought Timothy, at last. 'Well, I shall miss school and games and miss going to the circus and going out to tea if I don't do something about it. I shall have to stop being cheeky. It's a pity, because it made me feel so smart. But I can't have cheek going to my cheeks!'

He began to be polite in his answers. He didn't contradict. He didn't answer back. He didn't interrupt others, and bit by bit his balloon-like cheeks went down, until one day he looked quite himself again. The doctor came to see him and smiled.

'Ah – he's all right again now. He can go back to school. A most peculiar illness. I can't think what it was, even now!'

'It seems to have done him good, doctor,' said Timmy's mother. 'He's so quiet and polite now – quite a different boy. Not at all cheeky.'

The doctor laughed. 'You're right – he's certainly not CHEEKY any more. Let's hope he won't be, either.'

Well, the last time I saw Timothy, he had one cheek just a little bit swollen, but he was hoping nobody would notice. It was harder to get out of the habit of being cheeky than he had thought! Poor Timothy. He had a dreadful time, hadn't he, but if it taught him to be polite and well-mannered, it was worth it.

The Little Horse Tricycle

One fine sunny morning Paul went out for a ride on his little horse-tricycle. It was a nice little tricycle – a wooden horse on three wheels, and it went along quite fast when Paul pushed the pedals up and down with his feet.

Paul called the horse Spotty, because its wooden coat was painted with big, black and grey spots. It was getting rather old, and, one day, its long black tail had come out, which made Paul sad. A horse without a tail looks so strange. Paul tried to stick the tail back, but it all fell to pieces, and he had to throw it away. It was a great pity.

On this sunshiny morning, Paul thought he would ride to Bluebell Wood. So off he

went, pedalling down the road and then along the green path into the wood. And it was there that his strange and exciting adventure began!

As he went down the path he suddenly came to a part of the wood he didn't know at all. Queer, crooked little houses stood in a twisty street, and there was a large-windowed shop in the middle, with the strangest bottles of sweets, the queerest cakes and funniest buns he had ever seen. Paul stopped Spotty, his horse, and looked in at the window.

Then things began to happen. A pixie, with long pointed ears, rushed up, went into the shop, snatched up a bottle of sweets and a big chocolate cake, and then ran straight out again.

The shopkeeper at once appeared at the door, and shouted loudly: 'Stop thief, stop thief! You haven't paid me!'

But the pixie with the pointed ears ran off down the street as fast as ever he could. The shopkeeper, who was a gnome

with a red and yellow tunic buttoned up to his throat, danced about in rage – and then he suddenly saw Paul there, staring in surprise, sitting on his little horse-tricycle.

'After him, after him!' shouted the shopkeeper, at once. 'Go on, boy, go after him and catch him!'

The gnome jumped on to the horse behind Paul, and pushed off. Spotty the horse began to go fast, and Paul's feet flew up and down on the pedals. His hair blew out, and he gasped for breath. Spotty had never, never gone so fast before!

'There he is, the thief!' shouted the gnome shopkeeper, and he pointed ahead. Paul saw the pixie running down a hill in front of them, still carrying the bottle and the cake. On flew the horse-tricycle, faster than ever before, down the hill, and Paul began to feel quite frightened.

'Don't you think we're going rather fast?' he cried to the gnome. 'Suppose we have an accident!'

'Oh, never mind about a little thing like that!' cried the gnome. 'Go on, faster, faster, faster!'

They rushed on, down the hill and up another. The pixie in front could run really very fast indeed. Paul felt quite surprised when he saw his legs twinkling in and out. He had never seen anyone run so fast before!

Suddenly they came to a big town. It was a strange town, for all the buildings looked as if they were built of wooden toy bricks. The trees had round, wooden stands, just like toy farmhouse trees, and Paul thought they would fall over at a touch!

The runaway pixie rushed down the middle of the street. There was a small pond at the bottom, on which white toy ducks were swimming. The pixie suddenly tripped over a stone and fell sideways, splash! into the pond. The chocolate cake disappeared into the water and the bottle of sweets fell to the ground and smashed into a hundred pieces.

A wooden policeman suddenly appeared
and ran to pull the pixie out of the water.
Then up came Paul and the gnome on the
wooden horse-tricycle, and, in their excite-
ment, they ran straight into the pond!

They knocked the policeman and the
pixie flat into the water, Paul fell in with a
splash, the horse rolled on to its head and
stuck there with its three wheels in the air,
and the gnome slid into the mud at the
edge of the pond and sat there looking
most surprised.

Paul climbed out and began to laugh.
He really couldn't help it, every one
looked so funny. Then, up came some
more policemen, and dragged every one
out, the horse-tricycle too.

'Now then, what's all this?' said the
biggest policeman of the lot, taking out a
large notebook.

The gnome brushed the mud off himself
and explained about the robber-pixie, and
how Paul had been kind enough to go
after him on his tricycle. The pixie began
to cry and was marched off between two of
the policemen.

Paul looked in dismay at his horse-
tricycle. It was very muddy and very wet.
He himself was the same. Whatever would
his mother say when he went home?

The gnome saw him looking unhappy and patted him gently. 'Don't worry,' he said. 'I'll take you to my aunt's. She lives nearby, and she will dry our clothes for us and brush off all the mud. As for your tricycle, don't worry about that either. I'll take it to a shop I know here and they will clean it up beautifully for you.'

'I'll take it,' said one of the policemen. 'I pass by the shop.'

So off he went, wheeling the tricycle, and the gnome took Paul to a crooked little house not far away, where his aunt, a gnome just like himself, lived. She was dressed in red and yellow, with a big green shawl over her head, and had the kindest smile Paul had ever seen. She listened to the gnome's story in surprise, and then made them take off their wet, muddy things. She wrapped them up in two old coats and sat them by her kitchen fire, whilst she dried their clothes.

She gave them ginger buns and hot cocoa, and Paul enjoyed it all very much. It was most exciting to sit in Toytown with an old gnome aunt fussing over him, and a gnome shopkeeper smiling at him over a steaming cup of cocoa. What an adventure!

Soon, his clothes were dry, and after they had been well brushed, he put them on again. 'Now, what about my tricycle?' he asked. 'It is really time I went home, for my mother will be wondering where I am.'

Just then there came a knock at the door, and, when the gnome's aunt opened it, what a surprise! There stood the policeman with Paul's horse-tricycle, all cleaned up, shining bright – and whatever do you think! The horse had a brand-new, long, curling tail! You can't imagine how fine it looked!

'It's got a new tail!' cried Paul, in delight. 'Oh, how splendid!'

'The man who cleaned it up thought perhaps it had lost its tail in the pond,' explained the policeman. 'So he gave it a new one, in case it had.'

'Please thank him very much,' begged Paul. 'Are you coming back with me to your shop, gnome? I really must go now.'

'Yes, I'll come,' said the gnome, and slipped on to the horse behind Paul once more. 'Good-bye, aunt, and thank you very much!'

Paul called out the same and off they went through the crooked streets of Toytown. When they came to the gnome's shop he went inside and came out with a bag of little toffee-sweets which he gave to Paul.

'Thank you for your help,' he said. 'Come and see me again some day. Follow that green path and it will take you out of the wood. Good-bye!'

Off went Paul, full of delight. A bag of sweets, a new tail for his horse – and a fine adventure to tell! What a lucky boy he was!

When he got home he told his mother all about his adventure in the wood, and at first she smiled and wouldn't believe him. But when she saw the splendid new tail on the horse, and tasted one of the gnome's toffee-sweets, she changed her mind.

'Well, it *must* be true!' she said. 'How exciting for you, Paul! Do let's go and see the gnome one day soon.'

So they are going next Wednesday – and I wish I was going too, don't you?

Eggs and Marbles

Jack and Jim were twins and they did everything together. They went to school together, played Red Indians together, ran races together, played marbles, and went bird-nesting with one another.

Their mother didn't mind anything they did except that she hated them to take the eggs out of the birds' nests.

'It makes the birds so sad,' she said. 'It is so unkind of you, Jack and Jim. You don't want the eggs. You don't collect them. You just find the nest, see the eggs, and take them. It isn't fair of you. Let the birds have them – they don't belong to you, they belong to the birds.'

But Jack and Jim went on taking the eggs just the same. Their mother found

the bright, blue eggs belonging to the hedge-sparrow on the mantelpiece of the boys' bedroom. She was sad, because she loved the neat little brown hedge-sparrows that came about the garden in the winter.

'If you keep taking the eggs, we shall soon have no birds,' she said. 'Now listen – I will give you some beautiful glass marbles, if you will promise me not to take any more eggs.'

The boys loved playing marbles. They promised at once that they would take no more eggs. Their mother took them to a toy shop and bought them eight of the loveliest marbles you can imagine. They were very large, made of glass, and inside the glass were patterns of blue, red and yellow, curving like snakes. Jack and Jim were really delighted.

'Oh, Mother! Aren't they simply beautiful!' said Jack. 'The other children *will* think we are lucky to have these! They will be our very best marbles.'

The two boys were very proud indeed of

The little hen robin was indeed angry. The twins had robbed her first nest of eggs, and her second one as well. Now she had laid three more eggs in this nest, and she wanted to hatch them, and have the joy of seeing tiny nestlings cuddled in the cosy nest.

She flew right into Jack's face, and then flapped round Jim's head. The boys laughed. 'Silly little thing! As if *you* could stop us taking your eggs! We'll take them just to spite you.'

The two boys took the three little warm eggs from the nest. The robin was broken-hearted. She flew angrily round their heads, making such a noise that two big jackdaws flying overhead, came down to see what the matter was.

They found the little robin sitting on the edge of her nest. Her heart was filled with sadness. Her third batch of eggs was gone. It wasn't any good laying any more. She would have no little ones to feed and love that summer.

the wonderful marbles. They showed them to the other children, who tried to make the twins exchange them for sweets, chocolates or toys – but Jack and Jim wouldn't.

'No,' said Jack. 'They are the best marbles in the world. We shall never part with them. We shall keep them till we are grown up, and even then we won't give them away.'

The twins kept their word to their mother for a while, and did not take a single egg. Then, coming home from school one day, Jack saw a robin fly up from the ditch nearby.

'I bet there's a nest there,' he said, and he began to look. Sure enough, there *was* a nest, made of moss and dead leaves. In the nest were three pretty red-brown eggs.

'Robin's eggs,' said Jack. 'Let's take them.'

'We said we wouldn't,' said Jim. 'Look out – there's the robin come back. Hallo – it's angry!'

The jackdaws listened to all she sang to them. 'It's time we did something to stop those boys from robbing our nests,' said the first jackdaw. 'Do boys have eggs of their own? Shall we go and steal *their* eggs?'

The robin didn't know anything about boys, except that they stole eggs from her nest and from the nests of other birds. 'I wish you *would* steal their eggs, if they have any,' she sang, in her creamy voice. 'I wish you would!'

The jackdaws flew off. They saw the house the boys went into. They flew down to the roof. Then they heard the voices of the boys in the bedroom below.

'We'd better hide these robin eggs; Mother would be very upset if she saw them. After all, we did promise we wouldn't take any more.'

The jackdaws waited until they could no longer hear voices, and then they flew down to the window-sill of the bedroom. No one was there. They flew into the room, and walked about the floor, looking for any eggs that might belong to the boys.

'Look!' said the first jackdaw, suddenly. 'Eggs! Large, round eggs, all bright and shining.'

The other jackdaw looked. In a box, arranged on cotton-wool, were the eight beautiful glass marbles belonging to the boys. The big birds had no idea they were playthings. To them they seemed like big round eggs.

'These are the eggs belonging to the two boys,' clacked the first jackdaw. 'See the nest of wool they are in! We will take all the eggs away. Then they will not hatch and the boys will know what it is to feel unhappy.'

So, one by one, the jackdaws carried away the big glass marbles. They took them to their own enormous nest of sticks, high up in the church tower. There they put the eight wonderful marbles.

The twins came upstairs just as the jackdaws flew out of the window with the last

40

two marbles in their beaks. They gave a scream.

'Our marbles! Mother, Mother, quick! The jackdaws have taken our marbles. They're all gone! Mother, Mother!'

Their mother came running in. She looked at the empty box.

'Poor Jack – poor Jim!' she said. 'You know, jackdaws love bright, shiny things. They must have come along and seen your marbles, and taken them off. They once took a silver thimble of mine.'

'No, Mother, no, they didn't take our marbles because they like shiny things,' sobbed Jack, so upset that he couldn't help owning up to his mother. 'We broke our promise to you – we took some robin eggs – there they are, look, in this drawer – and I'm sure the jackdaws have come along and taken our marbles to punish us! We saw two flying overhead when we stole the robin eggs.'

Mother looked shocked and sad. 'To take eggs is horrid – but to break your word to me when I trusted you is dreadful,' she said. 'To think that my own two little boys should do that, when they love me and I love them!'

She didn't say any more. She went downstairs by herself. The boys were dreadfully upset, because they really did love their mother. They rushed after her to comfort her.

'We'll never do it again!'

'You can trust us, you can really!'

'We're awfully sorry. Forgive us and give us another chance, Mother. Don't look like that!'

'Of course I'll forgive you and give you another chance,' said their mother. 'But I'm afraid you've lost your marbles.'

They had. They are in the nest of the jackdaws, high up in the church tower – but they haven't hatched yet!

The Foolish Green Frog

There was once a green frog who used to float in Peter's bath every night. He was a nice little toy frog, and he and the toy goldfish swam together for Peter and made him laugh.

One day, Peter took the toy frog out into the garden with him. He played with it for a little while and then he threw it on the grass. When it began to rain he ran indoors and left the frog by itself.

The frog didn't like the rain. It was afraid that its nice green paint would come off. So it hopped away under a bush. And there it met a big thrush, turning over some moss to hunt for snails.

'Hallo!' said the thrush in surprise. 'What are you doing here, little frog? I thought all good frogs lived in ponds in the springtime.'

'Is that so?' said the little frog. 'Well, I will certainly go and live in the pond, too.'

'Shall I show you the way?' asked the thrush, politely. 'You are not very big, so perhaps you are not old enough to know the way.'

'I can find it by myself, thank you,' said the frog, haughtily. 'I am quite big enough. Good-bye!'

He hopped off to look for the pond. He longed to be a proper frog and not a toy one. He wanted to play with other frogs and have a good time.

But he didn't really know what the pond was like, so after a bit, when he met a garden snail he stopped and spoke to him.

'Good-day,' he said, 'could you tell me if I am anywhere near the pond?'

'Well,' said the snail, looking all round, 'that looks like it over there, doesn't it!'

The snail pointed with his horns to a large puddle on the path. The snail was very small and to him the puddle was as large as a pond. The frog took his word for it and at once leapt over to the puddle. He lay down in it, hoping that very soon he would see one or two real frogs to play with. But he didn't.

The sun came out and shone warmly, and very soon the puddle began to dry up! Then the frog found himself lying on a dry path, and the thrush, who came flying by at that moment, laughed loudly.

'Did you think that puddle was the pond?' he cried. 'Oh, you funny little fellow! That was only a puddle, and now it is dried up, so if you don't move someone will come along and tread on you!'

The frog hopped off quickly, angry with the laughing thrush. Soon he came to a big old sink, lying on the ground full of water. The gardener had put it there for the hens to drink from, but the little frog felt sure it was a pond. So into the old sink he hopped and swam around looking for more frogs to play with. But he didn't find any.

Soon, along came two big hens to have a drink, and they clucked loudly when they saw the little green frog.

'A frog in our drinking-water! Think of that! Let's drink him up!'

They pecked at the frightened frog, but he sprang out of the old sink and hopped away. One hen hit him with her beak and made a dent in his shoulder. He didn't like it at all.

On and on he went, and at last came to a big rain-barrel into which dripped water from the roofs. Beside it was a worm, poking his head out of a hole.

'Good-day,' said the frog. 'Can you tell me where the pond is?'

'What is a pond?' asked the worm, in wonder, for he had never left his little hole in all his life.

'Oh, it's a lot of water,' said the frog.

'Dear me, then, that must be the pond in this great barrel you see,' said the worm. 'I once heard a robin say that it was full of water.'

'Thank you,' said the frog, and you should have seen him making his way up the side of the barrel! It was quite exciting to watch him, and the worm felt certain he would tumble off and bump his head on the ground. But he didn't. He reached the top in safety and dived into the water that filled the barrel.

There were no other frogs there. It was most disappointing. The little toy frog swam about and then he suddenly saw a big face looking at him. It was the cook, coming out to get a pailful of water from the rain-barrel, and she *was* surprised to see a frog there!

He was so frightened that he leapt straight out of the rain-tub and fell to the ground.

'What are you doing in our rain-barrel!' cried the cook. Then he knew that he

hadn't been in the pond after all. On he went again – and at last he really did come to the pond!

But it wasn't the frog-pond – no, it was the duck-pond! No frogs live in duck-ponds for the ducks eat every one that they find. But the little toy frog didn't know that. He was so anxious to be a real, proper frog that he didn't think of any danger, but jumped head-first into the duck-pond and swam about to find some friends to play with.

But the only creatures there were the big white ducks! They saw him, and thinking he was a real live frog, they all came swimming up.

'Here's a frog!' they quacked. 'Here's a frog! Let's eat him! Oh, what a fine morsel!'

The frog was frightened almost out of his life! He must run away quickly before these big white birds pecked him and swallowed him. Out of the pond he jumped and all the ducks waddled out of the water after him.

Then suddenly something swooped down on him from the air and snapped him up – and off he went into the air to the sound of flapping wings! At first he thought that a duck had caught him, but soon he heard a chuckle and knew that it was the thrush who had offered so politely to show him the way to the pond.

'Well,' said the thrush, 'you've made a pretty mess of things, haven't you? I've watched you, and how I've laughed! I saw you in the puddle, and I saw you nearly drunk by those hens. I watched you climb into the rain-tub and how I chuckled when you sprang into the duck-pond! I was just in time to rescue you!'

'Oh, thank you,' said the little green frog gratefully. 'I'm sorry I was rude to you at first. Where are you taking me to?'

'Well, don't you want to go to the frog-pond?' asked the thrush.

'Not now,' said the frog. 'I've learned my lesson. I'm not a real frog and I never

will be. I'm only a toy frog and I'd better try to be what I'm meant to be – something for a little boy to play with. Will you take me back to Peter?'

'You'll just be in time for his bath!' said the thrush. He flew in at the open window and dropped the frog from his beak. Splash! He fell into a bath of warm water, and a little voice cried out: 'Oh, look! Here's Froggy back again! Oh, wherever did he come from?'

It was Peter, having a bath! He *was* so pleased to see the little frog, and as for the toy gold-fish he nearly went mad with joy to see his friend once more.

'I shall never try to be grand again,' thought the toy frog, swimming happily in the bath. And as far as I know, he swims each night there still!

Bom the Little Toy Drummer

Once upon a time there was a little toy drummer called Bom. What a fine noise his drum made as he beat it for all the toy soldiers to march to!

'Bom-diddy-bom-diddy-bom-bom-Bom! Bom-diddy-bom-diddy-bom-bom-Bom!'

Bom and the soldiers lived in a fine toy fort. It had strong wooden walls and a drawbridge that could be let up or down.

Captain Bang was the chief of all the soldiers, and what a loud voice he had. 'QUICK-MARCH! LEFT-TURN! HALT!' Bom was rather scared of him. But he liked Captain Bang's horse. He was called Thunder because of the noise his hooves made as he galloped round the fort.

Captain Bang was very proud of his soldiers – but he wasn't at all proud of little Bom. Bom was the smallest of them all, and, alas, he wasn't very brave.

He was afraid of guns, and when Captain Bang tried to teach him to shoot, Bom shook with fright.

'Now, now,' said Captain Bang. 'Aim straight – fire!'

And, goodness me, BANG went the gun – and shot off Captain Bang's bearskin hat!

'Try again, Bom,' said Captain Bang, 'and DON'T point the gun at me!'

So Bom tried again – and this time he shot off the top of the flag-pole! And when Captain Bang tried to teach him how to use the toy cannon – BANG! Bom shot off the top of one of the wooden towers! Away it went and toppled down outside the fort.

Captain Bang was so angry that poor Bom ran to hide in a sentry-box.

He wasn't much good at drilling either.

'QUICK-MARCH!' shouted Captain Bang, and away went all the soldiers in a fine row, with little Bom at the end. Then Captain Bang shouted 'LEFT-TURN!'

But Bom turned sharply to the right, and bumped hard into the soldier next to him – and down went the whole row like a set of dominoes! How the soldiers in the sentry-boxes laughed! But Captain Bang was in a fine temper.

'Shut Bom up in the fort till he grows a few brains!' he shouted.

'Guard, take Bom away and lock him up!'

All the soldiers stared at poor trembling Bom. One of them felt very sorry for him. He was Tan-Tara the trumpeter, Bom's best friend. He was sad when the guard came up and led Bom away to the little cell kept for bad soldiers.

Bom was sad too. He didn't like the tiny cell with its small bed and chair, and its little barred window. He sat on the edge of the hard bed feeling very miserable.

But suddenly he heard the toy army band – and the sound of his drum too! 'Who is beating my drum?' he said, and he put the chair under the barred window and peeped out. Yes – it *was* his beloved drum – Bom-diddy-bom-diddy-bom!

Tan-Tara the trumpeter saw Bom peeping out of the cell window, and he was sad for him. So he went to Captain Bang, sitting so grandly on Thunder, and saluted him.

'Sir!' he said, 'may the guard take Bom's drum to him, so that he can practise on it while he's in the cell?'

'Very well,' said the captain. So the next morning when the guard went to take Bom his bread and water, he brought the big drum too. How happy Bom was!

'My drum!' he cried. 'Oh, now I can practise my drumming and march all round my cell!' And round and round he went with his drum, Bom-diddy-bom-diddy-bom-bom-BOM!'

Bom didn't like being locked up all by

himself. He wondered how he could escape – and suddenly an idea came to him!

'I'll get inside my big drum and hide there!' he said. 'And when the guard opens my cell door I'll roll into him and bump him right over, and then away I'll go inside my drum, rolling, rolling, rolling!'

Now there was a small door in the side of the drum, and little Bom squeezed through it. He was just getting inside when he heard the jingling of the guard's keys. Hurry, Bom, hurry!

The guard opened the door and looked into the cell – but where was Bom? He was gone! The guard stared round in wonder.

'Bom has escaped!' he said. 'Only his drum is here!' And then what a surprise he had – the big drum began to roll towards him, all by itself. It rolled – and rolled . . .

Then BUMP! The drum knocked the guard right over and he began to yell. 'Stop that drum, stop that drum!'

How the soldiers stared when the big drum came rolling by itself on to the parade ground!

'Chase that drum!' shouted the captain in surprise, and leapt on his horse, waving his sword. 'Little Bom must be inside!'

Then off went everyone after the drum, which was now rolling towards the gate of the fort. Would the drawbridge be up – or would it be down so that Bom could roll over it and escape?

Hurrah! The drawbridge was down, and Bom rolled safely out of the gate inside his drum! What a good thing the fort was built on a hill, because now the drum could roll very fast indeed!

Away it went, bumpity-bumpity-bump over all the stones in the road. Bom felt quite giddy, but the drum was really enjoying itself.

Now round the corner was Mr Apple with his barrow of fruit – and *how* surprised he was when a big drum rolled up at top speed and bumped into his barrow!

Poor Mr Apple shot up in the air with all his fruit – and then, dear me, what a sight to see pears and apples and bananas rolling down the road after the big drum!

Then gallop-a-gallop at top speed came Captain Bang and all his soldiers. 'Stop that drum!' he roared.

Down a steep hill went the drum with Bom inside, and then up another hill and down again, and up and then down rushed Captain Bang and his soldiers.

Round the next corner was a little pond with ducks swimming on it. And SPLASH! The drum rolled right into the pond, and the water rose high up, like a fountain!

The little ducks were scared. They waddled out of the water quacking loudly. The drum floated gently over the pond and rolled out the other side. Away it went again, down a lane, round a corner, going slower – and slower – and slower. Oh, dear – the captain and his soldiers will soon be here!

The drum was so tired that it rolled into

a ditch and lay there, quite still.

'I daren't get out,' said Bom to himself. 'I can hear the shouts of the soldiers. Oh, I hope they don't see my drum when they come by!'

Suddenly a little rabbit popped its head out of a burrow. 'What's this thing that has suddenly arrived?' it said. 'Come, brothers, and see it!'

Then out came all the little rabbits to look at the drum – Floppy, Whiskers, Scamper, Bobtail, Little-Paws, Jumpy, Frisky – how surprised they were!

One little rabbit hopped on to the drum, and all the others followed. They thumped on it with their hind feet because they liked the noise it made. 'Bom-bom-bom!' said the drum, as they thumped hard.

Then up galloped the captain on his great horse Thunder, with all his soldiers behind him. 'Where's that drum with Bom inside?' he shouted. 'It has rolled out of sight. Look for it, men!'

Well! Not one of them saw the big drum

lying in the ditch, because so many rabbits were sitting on it, quite hiding it with their little furry bodies.

Captain Bang shouted loudly to them. 'Have you seen a little drummer rolling by with a drum?'

'A drum? What is a drum?' shouted the little rabbits. 'No, we have seen nothing rolling by!'

'Bom has escaped us!' said Captain Bang, angrily. 'We'll catch him sometime, though!' He swung his big horse Thunder round with a clattering of hooves. 'Back to the fort!' he shouted, and away went all the soldiers!

Then the little door in the side of the drum opened, and someone peeped out – yes, it was Bom, our little drummer!

'Oooooh! Who are you?' cried the rabbits as he crawled out, stood up, and strapped on his big drum again.

'I'm Bom, the little drummer!' he said. He beat his drum loudly and sang to the rabbits:

March, little rabbits,
Away you go
Down to your burrow
In a long, long row,
Bom-diddy-bom-diddy-bom-bom-BOM!

And soon all the bunnies were marching in a row, heads up, whiskers straight! Down the burrow they went, and at last only little Whiskers was left.

'Come with us, little drummer,' he said, but Bom shook his head.

'No! I'm going to see the world! I'm going to have adventures! And everyone will know when I'm coming, because they will hear my drum. Listen!'

And away he went, banging on his big drum and singing loudly:

Bom-diddy-bom,
Here I come-come-come,
Bom-diddy-bom,
With my drum-drum-drum,
Bom-diddy-bom-
diddy-bom-bom-BOM!

The Cat
Without a Tail

In Cherry Road there were six houses side by side, and in every house there was either a dog or a cat or both.

There was Scamper the terrier, and Tiddles the tabby. There were Smut and Soot, two black cats so alike that hardly anyone knew the difference. There was Scottie the Scottie dog. There was Tinker the mongrel. He was just a mixture of a lot of dogs. And there was Ginger the cat, whose coat was the colour of marmalade.

Now one day a new cat came to the house whose garden backed on to the six houses in Cherry Road. At first the other cats, sitting on walls or fences, only just caught a peep, but they said she looked a nice little cat. They thought they would like to know her.

But the new little cat was shy and frightened. She didn't seem to want to make friends. She vanished indoors as soon as any other cat appeared, and as for dogs, she was really scared of them.

The dogs and cats of Cherry Road talked to one another about the new cat.

'She's grey,' said Scamper the terrier.

'She's small,' said Smut and Soot.

'She's got a very tiny mew,' said Tiddles the tabby.

'Her eyes are green,' said Scottie.

'She's the only animal in that house,' said Ginger, the orange-coloured cat.

'I'd like to chase her,' said Tinker the mongrel.

The cats turned to stare at him, looking down their noses scornfully.

'You *would*!' they said. 'You have no manners. You are a common little mongrel.'

'Mongrels should be seen and not heard,' said the dogs. 'In fact,' said

Scottie, 'I think it's a pity they should even be seen, or smelt.'

'You're always horrid to me,' said poor Tinker. And so they were. He had tried to make friends with each one in turn, but they all turned their noses up at him. Smut and Soot were friends, of course. Tiddles and Scottie were firm friends too, and often slept in the same basket together. Ginger and Scamper were friends, though they did not live in the same house. Only Tinker had no friend.

The other cats and dogs thought he was a horrid, common little dog. He was a merry fellow, always wanting to play, and as sharp as could be. But none of the others would have anything to do with him at all. So poor Tinker had to run round and round after his own tail when he wanted a game, which was fun at first, but boring after a while because he couldn't help knowing that his tail grew on the end of himself.

Now, the very next day, the little new cat jumped up on to the sunny wall that divided her garden from the one at the back. All the other cats and dogs ran to speak to her – but as soon as she saw them, down she jumped and ran for the house as fast as she could.

But not before the animals had seen something very queer indeed.

'She hasn't got a tail!' said Tiddles, uncurling her beautiful grey one.

'I thought that too,' said Scamper, wagging his.

'How very peculiar!' said Smut and Soot.

'Poor, poor thing – someone must have bitten it off,' said Ginger.

'A dog must have chased her,' said Scottie. 'A dog that knew no better.'

'Yes, and that dog must be Tinker,' said Scamper at once. 'Didn't he say he would like to chase the little new cat? Disgusting animal! First he chases the poor creature,

then he bites off her tail! I vote we don't speak to him any more.'

'Not a word!' said Smut and Soot.

'I always did say he was a horrid, common little mongrel,' said Tiddles.

'So did we,' said Smut and Soot.

Just then Tinker ran up, wagging his tail. 'Woof,' he said. 'What do you think? The butcher's boy . . .'

Then he stared in astonishment – for all the cats and dogs put their noses into the air and walked off. Not one mew or bark could Tinker get out of them. He was puzzled and unhappy.

'What's the matter?' he barked. 'What have I done now?'

'Don't you dare to bark to us!' yowled Tiddles. 'We don't talk to dogs who chase little new cats and bite off their tails.'

'I didn't. I didn't!' yelped Tinker. But nobody believed him.

'Fibber!' said Ginger, and hissed.

'Story-teller!' said Scamper, and wuffed. 'Go away. We don't want to have any more to do with you.'

Poor Tinker. He was very sad. He

found that the cats and dogs really did mean what they said, and it wasn't a bit of good going to them and begging them to talk to him. So he kept away, and put his tail and ears down, feeling very unhappy.

One day he went to the bottom of the garden and lay down sadly, wishing his mistress would move, so that he might make a friend somewhere else. 'Though I do believe no one will ever make friends with a funny-looking dog like me,' thought Tinker. 'My ears are too long. My legs are too short. My tail is too curly. I'm an ugly dog.'

'What's the matter?' said a voice above him. 'Why do you whine like that?'

Tinker looked up. He saw the little new cat sitting on the wall. He put his head down on his paws with a grunt.

'Don't talk to me,' he said. 'You are the cause of all my trouble.'

'Why?' asked the little new cat.

'Because everyone says I have chased you and bitten off your tail,' said Tinker, gloomily.

'Well, you didn't,' said the little new cat, with a purr that sounded like a laugh.

'Who did?' asked Tinker. 'Nobody,' said the cat.

'Well, did you get it caught in a trap then?' said Tinker.

'No. I never had one,' said the little new cat. 'I'm a Manx cat, and Manx cats don't have long tails. I've just got a stump of a tail. Look. We never grow long ones.'

Tinker looked. He was very surprised. 'It's not very pretty to have no tail,' he said.

'I suppose not,' said the Manx cat. 'I'm always afraid of being laughed at or jeered at. So, as soon as I see any other dog or cat coming I jump away and go into the house. But it's very lonely, being somebody odd. You can never make friends.'

'I feel like that too,' said Tinker. 'You see, I'm only a mixture dog, a mongrel dog. I'm not a terrier or a spaniel or a bulldog – I'm a kind of mixture, and the

Tiddles. 'If he had, she wouldn't like him.'

'I'd like to be friends with her,' said Scamper, longing to join in the game. 'Sorry, Tinker, for saying things about you!'

'Well – you can play if you want to,' said Tinker, who was very forgiving. But the Manx cat didn't want to play with anyone but Tinker. She jumped up on to the wall and fled away.

'She's a bit particular about her friends, is little Shorty!' said Tinker, with a twinkle in his brown eyes. 'I'm rather particular too. I don't think I want anyone but Shorty.'

He strolled off and the others looked after him. They badly wanted to make friends with him now that he didn't seem to want them!

And after that Tinker had a grand time! He and Shorty became fast friends – and when she wasn't there to have a game, he could play with any of the others.

'And be careful I don't bite off *your* tails!' he would bark to them. 'Woooof! I'm after you!'

others don't like me. Now they won't speak to me because they say I chased you and bit off your tail.'

'How silly,' said the Manx cat. 'Do be friends with me. You are a bit ugly, but you've nice brown eyes and a lovely wag in your tail. My name is Shorty. What's yours?'

'Tinker,' said Tinker, joyfully. 'Come into my garden and play.'

So Shorty jumped down and soon she and Tinker were having a marvellous game of Round and Round the Raspberry Canes. They made such a noise that all the other animals came to see what it was.

'Tinker is friends with the little new cat!' said Ginger. 'I must say she looks a nice little thing, even though she's got no tail.'

'Tinker can't have bitten it off,' said

54

Dame Poke-Around

Old Dame Poke-Around came out of her cottage with her bag. She locked the door, put the key in her pocket and went to catch the bus to the next village. She was going to stay with her sister, Goody Grey-Hair.

The folk of Apple Village were glad to see Dame Poke-Around going away, even if it was only for a few days. They thought she was a mean, nosy old woman. She would never give a penny to anyone, nor even a bun to a hungry child. And she was always poking around, trying to find out things that people wanted to hide.

She knew when Dame Flip-Flap had a hole in her shoe. She knew when Mr Twink had forgotten to post Mrs Twink's letters. She knew when the little boys and girls over the way had been smacked and put to bed. Oh, she knew everything, did old Dame Poke-Around.

Nobody had ever known her do anything to help anyone. When Dame Flip-Flap lost her purse of money just at Christmas-time all the folk of the village joined together to give her the money she had lost – all except Dame Poke-Around. She said Dame Flip-Flap was a careless creature and deserved to lose her purse, and *she* wasn't going to give her a penny.

And when little Lucy Locket had whooping-cough badly, and had to be sent away to the seaside to get better, the village folk all gave five pence each to help her to pay for the journey – all except Dame Poke-Around, and she said Lucy Locket was making a fuss and didn't need a change at all.

So you can see that nobody minded when Dame Poke-Around went away for a week or two! The children especially were glad to see her go, for she scolded them whenever they played near her cottage.

Dame Poke-Around arrived at her sister Goody Grey-Hair's and settled in. She took the best bed and the biggest helping of everything, but Goody Grey-Hair was kind and generous and did not mind. Before Dame Poke-Around had been there three days, there came a knock at the door.

Goody Grey-Hair opened it. Outside stood a little brownie with a notebook, and pencil and a big purse.

'Please,' he said, 'I'm collecting.'

'What for?' asked Goody Grey-Hair.

'Well, a house has been burnt down in the next village,' said the little brownie. 'It belongs to an old woman, so we are all trying to get some money to pay for the house to be mended.'

'Dear, dear!' said Goody Grey-Hair. 'How sad! Well, I'll get my purse.'

'Oh no, you won't,' said Dame Poke-Around, coming to the front door. 'You won't give a single penny to the brownie. Is it a house in Apple Village that has been burnt down, Brownie?'

'Yes,' said the brownie.

'Well, that's the village *I* come from,' said Dame Poke-Around, 'and I can tell you there's not a single person there who doesn't deserve to have their house burnt down! Whose house was it, Brownie?'

'I don't know,' said the brownie. 'I belong to this village – I was told to collect money here for the old woman whose cottage was burnt down in Apple Village. All I know is that it was a grey cottage with roses at the door.'

'Hoo! That would be Dame Flip-Flap's!' said Dame Poke-Around joyfully. 'Well, she deserves her bad luck. Careless, lazy creature – always has holes in her shoes, and her hair flopping about her face! You just go and give all the money back that you've collected, Brownie, and tell people that the person you've collected it for isn't

worth it! The idea of mending up Dame Flip-Flap's old house for her! I shouldn't be surprised if she burnt it down on purpose!'

'Well, of course, if the person isn't worthy of having help, then I shall not collect money for her,' said the brownie, and off he went to give back the money he had already taken from kindly folk of the village.

Dame Poke-Around was delighted to think she had stopped people from giving money to help Dame Flip-Flap. She talked about nothing else all the time she stayed with Goody Grey-Hair, and really, her sister was quite glad when at last her stay came to an end, and she could see Dame Poke-Around off on the bus to her home!

Dame Poke-Around rode in the bus to Apple Village. She got off and walked up the street to her cottage. She had a look at Dame Flip-Flap's house to see how badly burnt it was – and to her great surprise it wasn't burnt at all! How strange!

But Dame Poke-Around got an even greater surprise when she came to her *own* grey cottage – for that was almost burnt down to the ground! Yes – the windows were gone, the roof was gone, and the front door was black and scorched. The walls had great holes in them – it was a dreadful sight!

'Oh! Oh! I forgot that my cottage was a grey one too – with roses at the door,' said Dame Poke-Around, in horror. 'It's mine that is burnt! Oh dear! Oh dear! Whatever shall I do?'

She ran to Bron's, the chief brownie's, and asked to see him. 'Oh, Bron!' she cried. 'My cottage is burnt down! What shall I do? I have no home – no money!'

'That is so,' said Bron, looking very grave.

'Won't the villagers help me?' cried Dame Poke-Around.

Bron shook his head. 'Dame Poke-Around,' he said sternly, 'when we knew your cottage was burnt, we went from house to house asking people to give money to help you – and my cousin, who lives in the next village, said he would ask people there. But when he came to your sister's cottage, and told the news, *you* thought it was Dame Flip-Flap's cottage that had been burnt – you said a great many unkind things. So my cousin gave back all the money he had collected and came to tell me why. And when I knew that it was *you* who were being so mean – you, for whom we were collecting so much money – why then I gave back all the money that *I* had collected! So there is none for you, Dame Poke-Around. Good-day.'

The old woman had the door shut in her face. She went down the street, weeping, and wondering what she should do. How foolish she had been! How mean! It was herself she had been mean to – and how horrid it felt!

As she passed Dame Flip-Flap's house the door opened and the kindly old woman looked out.

'Dame Poke-Around! I'm sorry your house was burnt down. You can come and stay with me a night or two if you like.'

'But I said such horrid things about you,' wept the old dame.

'Oh, never mind that,' said Dame Flip-Flap. 'You're in trouble, and that's all that matters!'

So Dame Poke-Around went to stay with Dame Flip-Flap, and my goodness me, didn't she learn a lot of things there – kindliness, cheerfulness, pity, generosity – it's no wonder she was a different person when she left the kindly dame and went to earn money to pay for the mending of her house!

And now the first one who opens her purse to any one in trouble is Dame Poke-Around. A good thing too, isn't it.

Pats of golden butter,
Little rounds of cheese,
Jars of yellow honey
Made by little bees.

Brown eggs for your breakfast,
Lettuce crisp and green,
Gingerbread and doughnuts,
Best you've ever seen!

'Oooh,' said little Bom, looking all round. 'What a lot of nice things to eat! Delicious fruit-pies! Fat sausage-rolls! And look at those crusty loaves of bread piled high on top of one another! I'll buy some.'

But, alas, when he turned out his pockets he couldn't find even a penny!

'*Now* what am I to do?' said little Bom. 'I know! I'll be like little Tommy Tucker! He sang for his supper – and *I'll* drum for my dinner! I'll sing for a loaf of bread.'

So Bom walked up and down in front of Mr Loaf's stall, and sang very loudly, beating his drum as he went.

Bom Goes to Market

Little Bom marched up hills and down for a very long way. 'Oh dear!' he said, 'I do feel hungry. I wish I had something nice to eat.'

Then in front of him he saw a signpost. 'What does it say?' said Bom. 'To Heigh Ho Market. I'll go there! Come along, Drum, left-right, left-right!'

And away he went with his drum to Heigh Ho Market. What a fine place it was! There were stalls everywhere, some selling fruit, one selling eggs, and another piled with big pats of golden butter.

Bom heard the market-people shouting their goods as they sold them, and he listened and laughed.

58

Baker, Baker, give me bread,
I've no money but instead
I'll play you tunes upon my drum,
Rumpti-tumpti-RUMPTI-TUM!

But, oh dear, how everyone jumped when they heard the drum – and what *do* you think happened at the last loud RUMPTI-TUM?

It was so very loud that all Mr Loaf's bread jumped up into the air with the sausage-rolls – and down they fell and rolled all over the place.

Mr Loaf was very angry. 'What's all this noise?' he cried. 'Be off with you – you've upset my loaves and my sausage-rolls too. Look at those dogs after them. Shoo, dogs, shoo!'

'I'll chase them off with my drumsticks,' said Bom, and he ran at the dogs and away they went, scared of little Bom's big drumsticks.

'And now please pay me for the bread and sausage-rolls those dogs ate!' said Mr Loaf.

'But I've no money, no money at all,' said Little Bom. 'I was just drumming for my dinner.'

'Hey – you're the drummer that Captain Bang is after!' cried Mr Loaf suddenly. 'Yes, you are! Catch him, quick!'

'No, no!' shouted Bom in fright, and away he went round the market with Mr Loaf after him. Look out, Mr Loaf – there's a bucket of milk just there!

But Mr Loaf didn't see it, and he stepped straight into it – and the milk spilt all over the place. Run, Bom, run, Mr Loaf is crosser than ever!

Bom ran into a shed where big round fruit baskets were piled up on top of one another. He stared at them.

'Oh, I've got such a good idea!' said Bom, and laughed. 'Now then, drum – I'll unstrap you – and put you down flat, like that – and then I'll pile these baskets on top of you, one by one, to hide you! No

one will notice you at the bottom of the pile!'

Certainly the drum was well-hidden. But what about Bom? He must hide too!

'I'll pop this big round basket over myself!' he said.

Mr Loaf and the market-people came into the basket-shed and looked all round. 'He came in here, I saw him!' said Mr Loaf. 'Hunt for him, the bad little drummer!'

But nobody guessed that Bom was under the big basket, and nobody saw the drum at the bottom of the big pile! They all ran out of the shed, shouting, and Bom peeped from under the basket to see if it was safe to go.

Yes, it was! But, oh dear, the basket was very tight, and Bom danced about trying to get it off – and just at that moment Mr Loaf came back and peeped into the shed again.

'Oh, the basket's alive, it's jumping about!' he yelled in fright, and away he went at top speed.

Bom wriggled free of the basket at last, knocked the big pile off his drum, and strapped it on again. Then out he crept, and went out of the market by a back way, not daring even to beat his drum.

But as soon as he came out on to the country lane again, he banged his drum loudly and sang:

The little birds sing,
The little bees hum,
But all I can do
Is to beat my drum.
I'm hungry and thirsty
And longing for tea,
But nobody cares
About me – me – ME!

Then suddenly Bom saw something away in the distance. It was a very tall tent, with flags flying all round it!

'It's a fair – or a circus!' said Bom. 'What fun!'

He soon came to a big circus in a field. There were big and little tents, and some cages and caravans too. There was a fine flag waving in the wind, and on it were three words: MR TOOT'S CIRCUS.

Inside the big tent everything was ready for the circus to begin. The clowns were there, and the horses. And Jumbo the elephant was there, carrying a bat in his hand to play cricket with his keeper.

But nobody was sitting in the seats. Mr Toots looked very worried indeed. 'Why doesn't Bill the gate-keeper beat his big drum to tell the people that the circus is about to begin?' he said.

One of the clowns came to tell him what had happened. 'Mr Toots, sir – Bill left the drum for a minute, and up came Jumbo the elephant – and he banged it hard with his cricket-bat – and, oh sir, he made an enormous hole in it, and now Bill can't beat the drum to tell the people to come to the circus!' said the clown, shaking his head sadly.

And just then what did Mr Toots hear in the distance but a big drum being beaten loudly! Whose drum is that? It isn't Bill's! It must be little Bom's!

'I can hear the bom-diddy-bom-bom of a drum – it's coming down the lane near-by!' cried Mr Toots. 'Look, it's a little drummer. He's come to the circus-gates! Quick, we'll borrow his drum to get the people here!'

So Mr Toots raced off to the circus-gates and shouted to little Bom. 'Hey,

you! You've come just at the right moment. Our drum is broken, look – lend us yours!'

'No,' said Bom at once. '*I'm* the only one that beats my drum!'

'Beat it yourself then!' said Mr Toots. 'We'll pay you well, little drummer, if you will beat it for us!'

Bom was surprised. He stood by the gate, raised his drumsticks and BOM – BOM – BOM, he began to beat his drum.

Then everyone in the nearby village heard it and cried out to one another: 'Quick! That's the circus drum! The circus is beginning. Let us go!'

Soon the road was full of people hurrying to the circus, while all the time Bom beat his drum and sang a little song very loudly indeed with Mr Toots and Bill the gate-keeper.

Come to the circus,
Come, come, come,
Come to the beat
Of my drum-drum-drum!
Elephants and monkeys,
Horses in a ring,
Clowns to set you laughing,
Hey dinga-dinga-ding!
Bom-diddy-bom, diddy-bom-bom-BOM!

Mr Toots was delighted when he saw that every one of his circus seats was full. He stood in the big ring cracking his whip, while his beautiful horses went round and round. Their feathery plumes nodded and

waved and they swished their beautiful long tails. How the audience clapped.

What a wonderful circus it was! Bom stood and watched it all through, and he was very sorry when it was over.

It was dark by then, and the stars were out in the sky. Little camp-fires were burning here and there, their flames leaping high. The circus folk were cooking their supper.

Bom was very, very hungry. He sat on his drum, wishing that he had some supper too. But perhaps Mr Toots will pay him for his drumming, and then he will be able to buy some food!

'Bom! Bom!' called Mr Toots. 'Where are you? Ah – there you are! Come and have supper with us by our camp-fire – and see, here is five pence to pay you for your fine drumming! You shall stay with us till Bill the gate-keeper gets his drum mended.'

Bom felt very happy. He sat by a lovely camp-fire, and what a fine smell came from the pot swinging over it! Everyone was very kind to him – but soon he felt very, very sleepy.

'I can't eat any more, thank you,' he said. 'I just – want – to go to – sleep!'

And he fell fast asleep cuddled up by his drum, with the camp-fire dying down, and the stars still shining high in the sky. Good night, little Bom – dream of your next adventure when you will be out again with your little drum, singing your song . .

Bom-diddy-bom,
Here I come-come-come,
Bom-diddy-bom,
With my drum-drum-drum,
Bom-diddy-bom-diddy-bom-bom-BOM!

Peter's Birthday

Peter woke up on his birthday and saw the sun shining brightly in at his window. He sat up joyfully.

'Proper birthday weather. I'm nine to-day – and Dad always promised me a bicycle when I was nine. I do wonder if he has remembered.'

He dressed and went downstairs – and the very first thing he saw, glittering and shining outside on the verandah, was a brand new bicycle! Peter rushed to it in delight, shouting at the top of his voice.

'Dad, you remembered! Oh, what a beauty!'

'Happy birthday, Peter,' said his father and mother, both together. Then his father stopped him from getting on his bicycle to ride round the garden.

'Now wait a moment. Before you even get on that bicycle, you've got to read every bit of what the Highway Code says about cyclists! Every word – and you've got to remember it too!'

Peter looked sulky. 'Oh blow! What's the sense of that? I've learnt to ride already, and I know all about the traffic lights, and putting my hand out to go round corners and things like that.'

'And before you go for your first ride *I* want to say a few things,' said his mother. 'You're so hasty and careless, Peter, and I want to be quite sure you know everything you ought to know before you go out riding.'

'Oh, Mother – don't lecture me on my birthday,' groaned Peter. 'It's going to be such a nice day with cards and presents – and my party this afternoon, with a birth-day cake and ices! Balloons and crackers! Smashing!'

His mother laughed. 'I'm not lecturing

you, you silly boy. It's a mother's duty to tell her children the rules of the road when they first have a bicycle. Well, I'll tell you after breakfast. Come along now, and see your cards and other presents. You can read the Highway Code before you go out.'

Well, after breakfast the telephone bell rang and his mother went to answer it. His father was going round the garden with the gardener. Peter stood impatiently in the hall, wishing he could go for his first ride.

'I'll just get on my bike and ride down the road and back,' he thought, getting tired of waiting. 'I can't possibly come to any harm! I've ridden round Ned's garden hundreds of times, and I shall be quite safe on the road!'

So he jumped on his bicycle, rode round the garden path, and out of the gate, feeling very happy. His own bright, shining bike! It was wonderful. He rang the bell loudly to tell a dog to get out of the way. He put his hand out to show everyone he was about to go round the corner. He stopped at the traffic lights because they showed red.

It was fun to be out on the road with cars and lorries all about. Better than riding round and round a garden! Peter began pedalling up the steep hill outside the town. He puffed and panted, and then he saw, just in front of him, a lorry going steadily up the hill. Peter pedalled hard to

catch it up and then caught hold of the back of the lorry. 'You can jolly well pull me up the hill!' he said to the lorry – and up he went behind it, not pedalling at all.

The lorry got to the top and came to the level again. Peter still held on, enjoying being towed along. And then things happened all at once, as accidents always do!

A dog ran in front of the lorry. The driver pulled up with a jerk. Peter's bicycle ran straight into the back of the lorry, and he fell off. A car behind didn't pull up in time and ran into the back of the lorry too. Poor Peter and his bicycle were between the car and the lorry.

What a to-do there was! The dog barked. The lorry-driver got down at once. The driver of the car leapt out. Peter was pulled out of the mess, with bits of broken bicycle sticking to him!

'Why, it's little Peter Brown!' said a woman. 'I'll go and telephone to his mother! Dear, dear – what a silly boy to hang on to the back of a lorry like that.

I'm surprised his father and mother didn't tell him the rules of the road!'

Poor Peter! His leg was broken and he had to spend his birthday in hospital. His bicycle was smashed to bits – his lovely new bicycle! He couldn't eat any birthday cake or pull any crackers.

'It's a dreadful price to pay for a minute's foolishness,' said his father, 'and a terrible way to learn to be careful!'

So it was. I'd rather read the Highway Code and listen to a bit of sound advice, than learn by smashing up my bicycle and my leg, wouldn't you?

Tig and Tag

Tig and Tag were two quarrelsome brownies. My goodness, how they squabbled! Sometimes it was really funny to hear them, because they shouted at one another for half-an-hour on end.

One day they went to fetch a basket of apples from Dame Twinkle. She had so many that she had said she would spare some for them. So they went off, very pleased to get them.

They took the basket from Dame Twinkle and thanked her politely. Then off they went home. On the way they met Snick and Snack, the two gnomes.

'Spare us an apple each, Tig and Tag,' said Snick looking longingly at the basket of rosy apples.

'No!' said Tig and Tag at once, both together. They were mean little creatures, and never gave anything away if they could help it. They went on, scowling. Snick and Snack winked at one another.

'If we can make them quarrel, we can take the apples for ourselves without Tig or Tag noticing,' said naughty Snick.

So they followed close behind the two brownies till they came to the hill that went up to the town.

'Look!' said Snick in a loud voice. 'Tig is letting Tag carry most of the weight of the basket! Isn't he mean! Up the hill too, just when they should both help fairly.'

Tag heard what Snick said and he stopped and glared at Tig.

'Snick says you are making me carry most of the weight,' he said. 'Please be fair, Tig, and carry your side of the handle properly.'

'I am!' shouted Tig.

'You're not!' shouted Tag.

'Now they're off!' whispered Snick to Snack. 'We can get close and take an apple or two without either of them noticing. Once they start to squabble they forget everything except their quarrel.'

'Yesterday you made me carry most of the washing-basket when we took it to Dame Feefo's!' shouted Tag.

'I didn't!' roared Tig.

'You did!'

'I didn't!'

'I say you did!'

'And I say I didn't!'

'Don't yell at me like that!'

'I'm not!'

'You are!'

'I tell you I'm NOT!'

'And I tell you you ARE!'

'You'll be sorry you spoke to me like this!'

'No, I shan't!'

'You will!'

'I won't!'

Snick and Snack grinned as they listened. They took two apples each from the basket. The quarrelsome brownies didn't notice. Some small pixies came up, and, seeing Snick and Snack helping themselves from the basket, they helped themselves too, standing and eating the apples whilst they watched Tig and Tag quarrelling.

'You're a long-nosed cucumber, that's what you are,' said Tig to Tag very rudely.

'And you're a red-faced tomato!' shouted Tag.

'I'm not!'

'You are!'

'I'm not!'

'Oh, be quiet!'

'Well, be quiet youself!'

'I shan't!'

'Nor shall I!'

'You want smacking!'

'So do you!'

'I don't!'

'You do!'

So the two quarrelsome brownies went on, squabbling hard, till quite a crowd came round them. And everyone helped themselves to apples, and stood munching round, watching. Tig and Tag didn't notice anything.

'I'll carry the apples home myself without your help,' said Tig.

'And I'll carry them without yours,' said Tag.

They both rushed for the basket – and, dear me, you should have seen their faces when they found it was empty! They stared round at all the crowd eating apples, and they shook their knobbly fists in rage.

'You've taken our apples!'

'Well, they were there,' said Snick. 'You didn't seem to want them, either of you. You shouldn't quarrel so. Then you could keep your eye on what belongs to you.'

'I hope you'll all have a pain in your tummies!' shouted Tag to everyone. And picking up the empty basket the brownies went sadly off home, making up their minds never to quarrel again. But, you know, I'm afraid they will.

As for Snick and Snack and the rest, they did have pains in their tummies, which really served them right, for they shouldn't have taken those apples!

Hallo, Rabbit!

'There's a new boy coming to school to-morrow,' said Bob to Timothy. 'I heard Miss Smith say so. Perhaps he will be jolly good at running and jumping, and we can have good games with him.'

'His name's Peter Jones,' said Timothy. 'He has come to live next door to us – but I don't think much of him, Bob. We do want a good runner and jumper, you know, to play leapfrog and that sort of thing. There are too many girls at this school! We want a few more boys!'

So Bob and Timothy looked closely at Peter when he came to school the next day. He had rather a pale face, sandy-coloured hair, and his legs were very thin. He didn't look as if he would be much good at anything, really.

At playtime the two boys went up to Peter. 'Come on, Peter!' said Bob. 'Let's have a game. Race you round the playground!'

'Well,' said Peter, 'I'd love it – but I can't run very fast.'

'Well, do your best,' said Timothy. 'Now then, one, two, three, go!'

Off went the three – but before they had gone very far, Peter stopped, and leaned against the wall to watch the other two.

'I can't run any farther,' he said when they came up to him.

'Well, you *are* a poor runner,' said Bob. 'Come on, let's play leapfrog.'

'I can't jump very well either,' said Peter, but he tried to leap over Bob when Bob when down. Over he went – and down he fell, knocking Bob over too.

'I told you I couldn't jump!' he said. 'I'm sorry, Bob – but I did tell you!'

'You *are* a rabbit!' said Bob, picking

himself up, and glaring at Peter. 'Fancy not being able even to play leapfrog. You're no use to *us*!'

Peter went red and turned away. Soon the school bell rang, and they all went in, boys and girls together.

At dinner-time Bob and Tim put on their coats and called to Peter.

'Coming along with us, Rabbit?'

'No, I'm going to stay at school for dinner each day,' said Peter.

'Whatever for?' cried the two boys in surprise.

'My mother says it's too far for me to walk home and back again twice a day,' said Peter.

'Poor little sandy Rabbit!' said Bob, mockingly. 'Diddums then! Were his poor little legs too tired?'

'I do think you are horrid,' said Peter, and he turned away.

'Well, good-bye, Rabbit!' called Bob, and off went the two, chuckling together. Peter went in to the school dinner, very much wishing that he could have gone off with Bob and Tim. He would like to have told his mother all about his new school but he would have to wait until tea-time.

'What a silly little rabbit,' Bob said to Tim on the way home. 'Can't run! Can't jump! Too far to walk home! Let's call him Rabbit, shall we, Tim?'

'Yes, it's a good name for him,' said Tim. So Rabbit became Peter's name, and soon every one in the school caught hold of the nickname, and wherever he went, Peter heard the same thing: 'Hallo, Rabbit!'

He was good at school-work and his teachers were pleased with him. He never minded helping anyone else, and the girls and some of the younger boys liked him very much. But Bob and Tim still laughed at him, and tried to make him race with them just for the fun of seeing him stop and say, 'I can't!'

On the day of the school sports all the boys and girls were very excited. There

were to be running races, jumping, three-legged race, egg-and-spoon race and an obstacle race. What fun!

'You must all be here at half-past two,' said the teacher. 'The sports begin at three, and your parents will be here then.'

So every one came at half-past two, and went into the sunny field, where Miss Smith had lists of the races and was telling everyone what to do.

'I'm in for every single race!' boasted Bob. 'How many are you in for, Rabbit?'

'I'm not going in for anything this year except the egg-and-spoon race,' said Peter. 'My mother says I can go in for everything next year.'

'Poor old Rabbit!' said Bob. 'Poor dear old spindle-legs! Was he afraid of falling over then? Won't the spoon be too heavy to carry?'

'I wish you wouldn't be so horrid,' said Peter, and he went red and walked away.

'Good-bye, Rabbit!' sang out Tim. But Peter didn't answer.

The sports were great fun! And who do you suppose won the egg-and-spoon race? Why, Peter did! The spoons were very small and the eggs were rather big – so most of the boys and girls dropped theirs – but Peter's hand was very steady, and although he ran very slowly indeed he managed to get to the winning-post before anyone else.

'Well, you needn't boast about your winning *that* feeble race!' said Bob. 'It's a girl's race, *I* always think! Girls have to do such a lot of sewing and knitting and they're used to keeping their hands steady! I wouldn't want to win that race!'

At the end of the sports all the children cheered their teachers, their parents and the school. Then they took their prizes and went home. Bob and Tim had seven prizes between them, so they were delighted.

'Look at this!' said Bob to Peter, and he showed him a brand-new purse. 'I won that for the long jump. And the prize for the high jump was twenty-five pence, and I won that too – so I have put the twenty-five pence into the purse, and I am going to spend it all on my mother's birthday next week! What do you think of that?'

'Won't your mother be pleased!' said Peter. 'I hope next year I'll win some money too – because my mother's birthday is in a fortnight's time.'

'Well,' said Tim, 'It's time we went home. Come on, Bob. I suppose you won't come with us, Rabbit – we are going to run.'

'No, I'll come by myself,' said Peter. 'Good-bye.'

Off went Bob and Tim and Peter walked slowly behind them, down the long street. Soon Bob and Tim were out of sight – and how Peter wished he could run as fast as they could! He would soon be home then!

As he turned the corner, he saw something lying in the gutter. He went to pick it up – and what do you suppose it was? Why, it was the fine new purse that Bob

had won at the sports! Peter opened it – yes, there inside were the twenty-five pence too! Bob must have dropped it without knowing as he ran home.

'He *will* be upset!' thought Peter to himself. 'I wonder if Tim would take it round to Bob this evening after tea. I could slip in next door and ask him. Then Bob would know that his purse and money were safe.' So after he had had his tea, Peter ran to the house next door, where Tim lived, and asked for Tim. When Tim came, he told him about the purse he had found.

'Poor old Bob! He will be upset when he gets home and finds he's lost it,' said Tim. 'Well, you can give it back to him at school to-morrow.'

'I wondered if you'd like to take it to him to-night,' said Peter. 'He might be worrying about it.'

'Oh, I can't do that,' said Tim. 'I'm tired after all those sports. I've got a nice new book and I'm going to read it and have a

quiet time. Bob won't mind waiting till to-morrow.'

Peter went back to his house, and looked at the purse. He knew quite well that Bob would be worrying very much over his lost money. Bob was fond of his mother and loved nothing better than to give her things, and do things for her. Peter guessed that he had been making all sorts of fine plans about spending his twenty-five pence on his mother's birthday.

'I've a good mind to take the purse round to him myself,' thought Peter. 'It's a pity he lives so far away – right at the other side of the steep hill. But perhaps I can catch a bus back. I've still got my last week's Saturday ten pence!'

His mother was out, so Peter told the maid where he was going, and set off. It certainly was a long walk, but at last the little boy reached Bob's house. He walked up the path and knocked at the door. Bob's mother came – and she said Bob was in the garden. So Peter went through the house and sure enough, there was Bob, sitting on a seat, looking as gloomy as could be. Peter thought he looked as if he had been crying for his eyes were red – and he guessed it was about the lost purse. He *was* glad he had brought it back to Bob!

'Hallo, Rabbit!' said Bob, in the greatest astonishment. 'Whatever have you come for?'

'Bob, I found your purse with the twenty-five pence in,' said Peter, and he held it out to Bob. 'I knew you'd be worrying, so I brought it back for you. Here it is.'

Bob took it, a big smile coming over his face at once. He went red with delight, and shouted for joy.

'Three cheers! I thought it was gone for good! I say, Rabbit, it *is* nice of you to bring it back! You can't think how glad I am! I've been worrying about it all the time!'

'That's all right,' said Peter. 'Now I must go, Bob, because I'd like to catch the bus back.'

'Did you walk here?' asked Bob.

'Yes,' said Peter.

'Well, I'd never have thought you would have done that!' said Bob, in surprise. 'It's such a long way. And you aren't any good at running or things like that.'

'Well, you see—' said Peter, and then he stopped.

'Well, what?' asked Bob.

'Well – I broke my leg last autumn – and I can't seem to run and jump as I used to,' explained Peter. 'But my mother says if I take things easily, and don't try to do too much, I shall soon be able to do everything well again.'

Bob stared at Peter – and then he went very red indeed. He had never felt so ashamed of himself in his life! To think they had teased and jeered at Peter because he couldn't run and jump – and it was all because he had had a broken leg!

'Rabbit, I'm terribly sorry that Tim and I were so horrid to you,' he said. 'We didn't know.'

'You didn't give me a chance to tell you,' said Peter. 'Besides, I hate making excuses. I knew that I should be able to run and jump as well as you can in time. So I waited.'

'You're a real sport!' said Bob, and he flung his arm round Peter. 'Will you be our friend? We always wanted a good sport to join us in our walks and games. Will you forget our horridness and be friends?'

'I'd love to!' said Peter, his face shining. 'My, won't we have some fine times together! You can come and play with my steam-train. I've been longing to show it to you. Oh, we'll have great times together.'

'And we won't call you Rabbit any more!' said Bob.

'Oh, but I like it!' said Peter. 'I don't mind a bit. I know I'm not a real rabbit, you see – someone really feeble and weak. I'll be as strong as you are soon! Call me Rabbit all you like – *I* don't mind!'

So Peter is still Rabbit – and now you should see the three of them together! They are the very best of friends, and Peter's legs are getting fat and strong again. I shouldn't be at all surprised if he beats the other two at the sports next year – but *they* won't mind. They will cheer and say: 'Well done, Rabbit!'

That Tiresome Brownie

Farmer Straws was very angry. In his dairy there was a hidden brownie, and try as he would, the farmer could not find out where he was hiding.

'He sips my cream at night, drinks the milk, licks the butter and nibbles at the cheese!' raged Mr Straws. 'That tiresome brownie! Wait till I catch him!'

A little chuckle came from somewhere in the dairy, and the farmer glared round him. Where *could* that brownie be? It was most peculiar, really. Mr Straws had looked in every corner, in every pail, in every churn. He had run his hand along every shelf, and had even climbed up to the rafters and looked there. But not a thing could he see. There was no brownie to be found anywhere.

'I told you there was a brownie about, didn't I?' said the old cow-woman, Dame Milky. 'And didn't I tell you to put down a saucer of cream for him each night, so that he wouldn't get into the dairy and plague you? Ah, I know the ways of those brownies, I do. A saucer of cream, and they'll leave you alone – but neglect them, and they'll play you some fine tricks.'

'What I can't understand is where he hides!' said the farmer, scratching his head. 'I've looked everywhere!'

'Yes, it's a puzzle,' said Dame Milky. 'I've looked too – but I can't see him either – and all the time you hear that wicked little chuckle of his – ah, I'd like to get my hands on the little rogue, so I would! Master, why not go to Mother Buttercup and ask her to look for the brownie with those sharp eyes of hers? She's a rare one for seeing.'

So Farmer Straws went off to Mother Buttercup and begged her to come and tell

74

him where the brownie was hiding. She came at once, and peered round with her little sharp eyes. As she looked, a small chuckle sounded from somewhere. Mother Buttercup looked about at once – and then she nodded her head and turned to the farmer.

'You won't ever find that brownie,' she said. 'He can't be seen! He's invisible! He must have drunk some magic drink that makes him unseeable. Aha, Farmer Straws, he'll be there for the rest of his life and yours, tormenting you, and plaguing you! Why didn't you set down a saucer of cream for him as Dame Milky told you to? He would have been satisfied with that!'

She went off – and the farmer sat down on a stool and groaned in despair. It was bad enough having a brownie teasing him – but to have one that could never be caught because he couldn't be seen was worse still! If only he could get hold of him to give him one good slap!

'Aha!' said a small voice nearby, and that little brownie chuckle came again. The farmer turned – but, of course, he could see nothing at all.

He went to the farmhouse to his tea. His two children were there, sharp little monkeys, called Jack and Rosy. They saw their father looking gloomy and they asked him what was the matter. So he told them, with much shaking of his head.

'He's ruining me!' he groaned. 'The milk, cream, butter and cheese I have to throw away each day! You see, the brownie turns it sour when he touches it. It's no use for anything. Well, if this goes on, children, you won't either of you get those ponies you've been wanting!'

'Father! But you promised!' said the two children in dismay.

'Well, you think of some way to get hold of this brownie, my dears, and you can have your ponies!' said Farmer Straws, and off he went to feed his pigs.

'Father! Father! Will you promise to let us have our ponies if we get the brownie

for you?' Jack called after him.

'All right!' shouted back the farmer, and went into the pig-sties.

"*We* can't catch that brownie!' said Rosy, to Jack. 'If anyone could it would be old Mother Buttercup or Dame Milky – but *they* haven't done so!'

'Just wait a minute,' said Jack, his eyes gleaming. 'I've got an idea. I'm going shopping. Coming?'

Off they went. Jack went to the chemist and got five pence worth of snuff, or sneezing-powder. Then he went to buy himself and Rosy a pair of stout gardening gloves. Rosy could not think what he was doing!

'Wait and see!' chuckled Jack. 'I've got a fine plan!'

That evening, when the milking was done, and the cream was set out in bowls in the dairy, the two children crept in at the door.

'Shut all the windows,' said Jack, 'and I'll lock the door.'

This was done. Then Jack told Rosy to put on her pair of thick gardening gloves, and he slipped his on too. From somewhere in the dairy came a tiny chuckle. Jack heard it.

'All right, my fine fellow!' he called. 'I can hear you! You'll be caught in a minute!'

There came the sound of a louder chuckle and Jack grinned. No wonder that brownie had angered his father!

'Get out your handkerchief, Rosy,' whispered Jack. 'Hold it over your mouth. I am going to blow this sneezing-powder into every corner of the dairy – and then, my word, we'll have that brownie in our hands before we can say "Jack Robinson."'

Rosy held her handkerchief to her mouth. Jack took out the box of snuff and began to blow it into every corner.

And soon he heard the sound he wanted to hear. 'A-tishoo! A-tishoo!'

'He's over there!' said Jack, and the two

children rushed to the far corner. But the brownie slipped between their legs, and got away.

'A-tishoo! A-tishoo!' he sneezed, and again the two children rushed to the place where the sneezing came from. But once more the brownie escaped. The children could not see him, but the sneezing was so loud that they could always guess where he was as soon as he sneezed.

'A-tishoo! A-tishoo! A-tishoo!' sneezed the brownie, trying his best to stop his sneezing – but the more he tried, the worse it got! 'A-tishoo! A-tishoo!'

'Over there by the milk-churn!' cried Rosy, and off went the two children. They felt the brownie slip by them, and very nearly caught him that time.

'He's very small!' said Jack. 'We must put our hands down to get him next time.'

Jack blew out some more of the sneezing-powder, and at once they heard the brownie sneezing without stopping! 'A-tishoo! A-tishoo! A-tishoo! A-tishoo!'

'Over there!' shouted Jack, and the two children ran to the corner where the sneezing came from. Both put their hands down – and caught hold of a small, wriggling body!

'Got him!' cried Rosy. 'Hurrah!'

The brownie began to bite and scratch for all he was worth. Rosy was glad that Jack had thought of buying thick gardening gloves. She shook the naughty little creature hard, and cried: 'Now behave yourself! Let us see you, and maybe we'll bargain with you, and let you go!'

The brownie suddenly became still in their hands, and they looked down. He was beginning to be visible! He was gradually appearing before them. First his pointed, cheeky face, then his long arms, then his rounded body, and last of all his short, knobby legs. There he was – the wicked little brownie, grinning up at them, and once more trying to wriggle out of their hands.

'Let me go!' he said.

'Not till we've had a talk!' said Jack firmly.

'Now listen to me. We've got you, and if we hand you over to our father, you will get such a spanking! My, I wouldn't like to be you!'

'No, no, don't do that!' begged the brownie, really frightened. 'Let me go. I promise I won't plague your father any more. Just put down a saucer of cream for me each night, and I'll be good. I won't put so much as one eyelash into the dairy, I promise you!'

'No, not one saucer of cream do you get!' said Jack. 'You'll go right away from here, and you'll never come back! If you ever come round here again, I'll use my sneezing-powder, and hand you over to our father at once. I promise you that!'

'Just a little saucer of cream each night!' wailed the brownie.

'Oh, if you're going to be a nuisance, we'll give you to father straightaway,' said Rosy, and she made as if she were going to take the brownie out to the pigsties. He screamed and kicked, and tried to bite through her glove.

'That's enough!' said Jack sharply, and he gave the brownie a slap.

'I'll do all you say, I will, I will!' wept the naughty little creature. 'I'll go this very minute!'

'Off you go then!' said Jack, and he let the brownie slip from his hands. The small creature hopped out into the farmyard, and looked about to see which way to go. The farmer, coming out from his pigsties, saw him, and shook his fist at him.

'Same to you, same to you!' yelled the defiant brownie, and made a rude face at Mr Straws, who was too far away to get him.

But the farmer's dog saw him, and he came after the brownie with a loud bark. 'Wuff! Wuff!'

'Oooooooweeeee!' shrieked the little fellow in dismay, and hopped up on the wall. He ran along it, leapt into a bush, and disappeared – and that was the last they saw of that tiresome brownie!

'How did you find him?' Farmer Straws cried.

The children ran up and told him. Farmer Straws slapped his knee and roared when he heard about the sneezing-powder.

'A pretty trick, a pretty trick!' he shouted. 'Well, my clever ones, if that brownie leaves my dairy alone to-night, you shall have your ponies!'

The cream, butter and cheese were all untouched that night – so the children got their ponies, and very proud of them they are too!

As for the brownie, goodness knows where he went. If he should ever come to you, remember this – put a saucer of cream down for him each night, and he'll play you no tricks – but if you forget, you'll soon long to spank that tiresome brownie!

Bom at the Circus

Bom slept soundly all night long, cuddled beside his drum. He was so tired that he didn't hear the trumpeting of Jumbo, the big elephant, or the neighing of the beautiful circus horses as they went for a trot round the field.

But at last he woke up and rubbed his sleepy eyes. At first he thought he was back in the toy fort, but when he stood up and looked round, he remembered where he was – with Mr Toots' Circus!

'How busy the circus camp is!' thought Bom as he strapped on his big drum. 'Dear me – what a lot is going on! I'm hungry – I wonder if I can buy some breakfast with my five pence.'

'Hallo!' said a voice behind him. 'So you're awake at last! Go to my caravan and you'll find some sandwiches waiting for you.'

It was kind Mr Toots, and Bom was very pleased to see him. 'Oh, thank you,' he said, and off he went to find the sand-wiches. Then he wandered round the circus field, holding his two drumsticks in one hand and the sandwiches in the other.

He saw the lovely circus horses being exercised in a row, stepping out daintily – and as Bom watched them a little circus girl leapt up to a horse's back and galloped up and down the field.

'How clever you are!' shouted Bom, and the little girl waved to him. Then she suddenly stood up on her horse and there she was, galloping round the field, standing up all the time! How daring she is! 'I wish *I* could do that!' Bom thought. 'How clever these circus people are!'

'Hrrrrrrmph!' suddenly said a voice far above him. Bom looked up – and there was big Jumbo the elephant, waving his trunk over Bom's head!

'Oooh – don't tread on me, Jumbo!' said Bom. And then, what *do* you think Jumbo did? He took hold of Bom with his trunk and set him firmly on his great head – what a thing to do!

Bom was so surprised. The little girl riding on the horse galloped up and laughed.

'Take him for a walk, Jumbo. Take him for a walk!' she cried, and away lumbered the big elephant with Bom bobbing up and down on his head!

Everyone pointed at him and laughed. Bom laughed too. An elephant's head was such a queer place to ride on!

'Oh – I'm slipping, I'm slipping!' cried Bom suddenly. 'Help me, someone.'

'Slide down Jumbo's trunk!' shouted the little girl on the horse.

And Bom found himself sliding down the elephant's big trunk – whoosh, down he went to the ground – what fun!

It really was fun to be in a circus camp. Everyone was so kind to little Bom, and he liked them all. 'But I think I like the clowns best,' he thought. 'They are so very funny.'

There were four clowns in the circus, and they were most amusing. First there was Smiler, and you can see why he was called by *that* name. Surely no one ever had such a big smile before!

Then there was Binks. Binks was a most peculiar clown, because he liked walking on his hands better than walking on his feet. Look at him – he even wears his *hat* on his feet!

'You should see Binks go shopping,' said the little circus girl. 'He brings the basket home on his feet too. The only thing that makes him cross is when a dog runs up and licks his face – it's so near the ground that dogs love to do that.'

The other two clowns were called Biff and Bash, because they were always pretending to fight one another.

Biff! goes one, and Bash! goes the other, but as they only hit each other with

balloons it doesn't really matter.

'Pop! Pop! Pop!' went the balloons when they burst, and how Bom jumped!

'Hey Bom – you try to walk on *your* hands!' called Biff. So Bom took off his drum and tried, while Biff held his feet up in the air. Bom began to walk on his hands – but just then Biff let go his feet and poor Bom at once fell flat on the ground!

How everyone laughed! Bom laughed too. It really was fun to be with the four clowns.

'Try again,' they cried, but Bom shook his head. 'No – I think I walk better on my feet!' he said, and put on his drum again.

Smiler was very good at walking the tightrope. It was stretched from post to post – and there goes Smiler, walking to and fro, faster and faster!

'However *can* you do that?' said Bom, in surprise.

'Oh, it's easy,' said Smiler and jumped down. 'You try, Bom.' They put Bom on the tight-rope, and he stood there, wob-

bling. 'Oooh – I'm wobbling dreadfully,' he said. 'Steady me, Smiler!' So Smiler steadied him, and Bom tried again. But then he wobbled worse than ever – he's going to fall – catch him, Smiler!

Smiler caught Bom as he fell off, and all the clowns laughed. 'Well tried, little Bom!' said Smiler. 'Tight-rope walking needs a lot of practice!'

Then there was Long-Legs the stilt-walker. It was quite difficult to look right up to his head, he was so very, very tall. First you saw his feet, then his legs – oh, what long, long legs – then his body – then his neck, and last of all his head, very high up, wearing a tall top hat!

Bom didn't know at first that inside Mr Long-Legs' trousers were strong wooden stilts, and he really thought he must be a giant. How surprised he was when Mr Long-Legs took off his stilts, and became his real self!

'Oh, what a tiny little man you really are!' cried Bom. 'Why, you're no bigger

Bom loved the little circus monkeys too. There were five, all as mischievous as could be. They belonged to Madame Wooky, and she loved them all.

One always sat on her shoulder, dressed in a little coat and shorts. That was Bing, the most mischievous of the lot. He was always whispering in Madame Wooky's ear, and she nodded her head and listened.

'Does he tell you secrets?' asked Bom, in surprise, and Madame Wooky nodded and smiled.

'Oh, yes. That's how I know everything that goes on in the camp!' she said. 'Isn't it, Bing?'

Flick was another of the five monkeys. She was a pretty little thing who loved to dress up. She often went to Madame Wooky's caravan and borrowed one of her hats.

Janty was the third monkey and she always wore a scarf and shoes, and Dinky, the fourth monkey, had a little hat with a

than I am – and I thought you were a giant. Do let me try stilt-walking. It looks easier than some of the other things I've tried.'

So Mr Long-Legs let Bom strap on his long wooden stilts, and wear his long trousers – and now, what a surprise! Bom is as tall as Mr Long-Legs was, and he's walking along on the stilts, beating his drum and shouting:

Hear comes Bom
The Big Big Bom.
I've grown so high
That I bump the sky.
My shoes I can't see
For I'm tall as can be.
Here comes Bom,
The Big Big Bom!

How everyone cheered and clapped! 'You ought to join our circus and live with us, Bom!' cried Smiler. 'You're really very good.'

feather in, and a fluffy skirt. Trip was the last one, a smart little fellow, dressed just like a toy soldier. Bom loved to play with them all.

But now see what Bing has done, the mischievous little thing! He got hold of one of Bom's drumsticks, and leapt up on to the roof of Mr Toot's caravan, and drummed on it with the stick – just like Bom beating his drum! Bom-diddy-bom-diddy-bom-bom-BOM!

Mr Toots didn't like monkeys drumming on his caravan roof. He put his face out of the window and roared: 'Get off my roof, whoever you are!'

But Bing wouldn't move. He just went on drumming. Then Bom had a very good idea. He saw a big net nearby and picked it up. He stole up to the caravan and in a trice he had dropped the net over naughty little Bing. Down he came, well and truly caught.

But Bing wouldn't give up the drumstick. Bom took hold of one end and tugged and pulled – the two of them went to and fro, to and fro, and it was a real tug-of-war!

Then away went Bing with the drumstick up on the roof of a tent – and there he left the stick, standing upright in a corner. Bom was very angry.

'How can I beat my drum with just one drumstick?' he shouted.

But just then Madame Wooky came along and called to Trip, the little soldier-monkey. 'Trip! Fetch that stick! At once, please!'

And Trip, who was the most obedient of the five monkeys, leapt up on to the tent-roof and brought down the stick.

'Thank you, Trip!' said Bom, pleased. 'See – here is a toffee for you!'

And then – just at that moment – some-one gave a loud shout. 'Look! Look! Who is that galloping in the distance, coming nearer and nearer with others be-hind him?'

'Oh! It's Captain Bang and all his soldiers!' cried Bom in a fright. 'They're after me again. Oh, what SHALL I do?'

The Teddy Bear's Tail

The teddy bear was really tiresome. He was such a grumbler, and every day he seemed to find something new to complain about.

'I wish I could bounce,' he said, when he saw how well the ball could bounce. 'I do wish I could. I would bounce right up to the mantelpiece then, and see if I could take a sweet out of the tin there.'

Then another time he said: 'I do wish I had a key. The train has a key, and the clockwork mouse, and so has the clown. But I haven't. It isn't fair.'

When he saw the dolls sitting in a row, all beautifully dressed, he had another fine grumble.

'Look at those dolls!' he said. 'All with hats and coats and dresses and shoes! And I haven't any clothes at all. Not even a ribbon round my neck. It isn't fair. I've only got my skin.'

'You've got a nice *furry* skin,' said the pink cat. 'Don't grumble so.'

Then the teddy found something else to grumble about. He looked behind himself for the first time and saw that he hadn't got a tail! He stared in surprise.

'Where's my tail?' he said.

'You never had one,' said the black dog.

'Why not?' asked the bear. 'I'm an animal, aren't I? Then why haven't I a tail?'

'How should I know,' said the toy dog. He wagged his own black tail, looking pleased with it.

'I've got a tail too,' squeaked the clockwork mouse.

'So have I,' said the pink cat, and she swung it round to show the bear.

'Mine's the longest,' said the toy monkey, and flapped it in the bear's face.

'Don't,' said the bear, crossly. 'Oh, I do think it's terribly unfair. *Why* haven't I got a tail? Have I lost it?'

'I told you. You never had one,' said the dog, and he gave a giggle.

Well, after that the bear was dreadfully tiresome. He went on and on grumbling because he hadn't got a tail. At last the golliwog could bear it no longer.

One night, when the bear had gone out on to the landing outside the nursery door, he spoke to the toys. 'For goodness' sake, let's give the bear some sort of a tail. I shall go mad if I hear him wail because he's no tail.'

'Why does the teddy bear wail? Because he hasn't a tail,' said the pink cat at once, feeling clever. 'That rhymes.'

'Be quiet,' said the golliwog, wishing he had made up the rhyme himself. 'Now – who will give the bear his tail? Clockwork mouse, will you?'

'No,' said the mouse. 'I want mine.'

'Will you, black dog?' asked the golly. 'You've had yours for ages.'

'And I want it for ages more,' said the dog. 'I keep my wag in it.'

Nobody would give up their tail. It was very annoying. But at last the old kite in the toy cupboard spoke in his funny, windy voice.

'He can have *my* tail. I'm broken now, I shan't fly any more, and as I only use my tail when I fly, it's no use to me now.'

'Well – it's rather a funny tail,' said the golliwog, doubtfully. 'I don't know if it will suit a bear.'

'Don't ask him if it will suit him,' said the kite. 'Just give it to him. Tie it on him when he's asleep. He's always grumbling because he hasn't got one, isn't he? Well, make him have one, and tell him to stop grumbling.'

The toys giggled. They thought they would do that. It amused them to think of the teddy bear running about the nursery with an enormously long tail made of paper twists tied on to string! That was what the kite's tail was made of!

So, the next time the bear sat in a corner of the top cupboard to go to sleep, the golliwog snipped off the kite's tail, and neatly tied it on to the back of the teddy bear. He did it so gently that the bear didn't know it. He just lay there, fast asleep.

He woke up very soon and stood up. He thought he would go and have a run round the nursery with the clockwork mouse, who was busy running all round the hearth-rug. The golliwog had wound him up, and he was having a fine time.

So the bear stepped out of the top cupboard and began to run to the mouse. Rustle-rustle-rustle went something behind him, and he jumped in fright. He turned round quickly and saw, to his horror, that he had a long, long tail unwinding itself over the carpet.

'What is it?' he yelled.

'Your new tail,' said the golly, with a grin. 'You are always grumbling because you haven't got one, and we were so tired of hearing you – so the kite has given you his tail to wear.'

'I don't like it,' said the bear. 'Take it off!'

'What! After we have gone to all the trouble of putting it on you for a lovely surprise!' cried the pink cat. 'Ungrateful creature! Certainly we shan't take it off!'

The bear hated his new tail. For one thing it made such a rustly noise behind him. For another thing, it was so very long, and kept getting caught round table-legs and things like that, so that the bear spent half his time untangling it. Sometimes it tangled itself round his legs and made him fall over. He got very, very angry with it.

And then one day Donald, the little boy in whose nursery the toys lived, picked up his teddy, and was most astonished to see the long, long tail tied to him. He took it off at once.

'You've got all tangled up with the kite's tail!' he said. 'There – now you're all right.'

The bear was delighted. How lovely it was to run about the nursery at night again without having a horrid long tail rustling behind him and getting caught round everything. The toys looked at one another and smiled.

'Poor bear – sorry you've lost your tail,' said the golliwog. 'We'll get you another. A tale out of a book, perhaps.'

'I don't want a tail,' said the bear.

'Well, be careful you don't grumble again because you haven't something that other people have got,' said the golliwog. 'If you grumble because you've no whiskers we'll give you enormous ones made of the hairs from the mane of the rocking-horse!'

'And if you grumble because you've no key, we'll make a hole and fit the key of the clock there,' giggled the pink cat. 'Then you'll say tick-tock whenever we wind you up.'

'And if you grumble because you haven't any clothes to wear, we will dress you up like a baby doll and see how funny you look,' laughed the curly-haired doll.

'I shan't grumble any more,' said the bear, in rather a small voice. And he didn't. He was quite a nice bear after that – but there was one toy he would never, never speak to, and that was the old kite in the cupboard.

But you may be sure the kite didn't mind that!

Fred's Forgettery

There was once a boy who had a very bad memory. He didn't even *try* to remember anything, which made things even worse!

'Fred, you haven't got a memory, you've only got a forgettery!' his mother said to him, many times. 'Didn't I remind you three times to call at the shoemaker's for your shoes and *now* you haven't remembered!'

'Oh Mother, I quite forgot,' said Fred.

'But did you *try* to remember?' asked his mother. 'No, you didn't. Now you will have to wear your old shoes with your new suit when you go to see Granny. That really is a pity.'

One day the circus came to Fred's town. It really was a marvellous one. It was Mr

Phillippino's, and there were elephants, a giraffe, monkeys, and the funniest clowns you ever saw.

Some of the children went, and they really loved it. Fred wanted to go, but as he had really been very silly that week, his mother said no.

'You forgot to take your books to school yesterday, and lost a good mark for that,' she said. 'And on Monday you forgot I had asked you to stay at school to lunch and you came home, and made a great fuss because I was out and there was no one to get you your meal. And this very morning I asked you to call at the paper shop and bring me back my paper, and you didn't. No, you don't deserve a ticket for the circus. That forgettery of yours is playing all kinds of tricks this week!'

Now, on Thursday evening Fred had to go to a nearby friend's house to borrow a school book he had forgotten. As he came back with it he saw an old man hurrying to catch the post.

'The post has gone!' thought Fred. 'I saw the postman collecting the letters as I came by. The old man has missed the post.'

The man stopped by the pillar-box and looked at the post times, as he held up the letter to the slit in the red box. Then he gave a cry of annoyance, for he saw that there was no collection until the next day. He had missed the last post.

'What a nuisance!' Fred heard him say. 'Missed the post! Now the letter won't get there till Saturday morning if I post it. I'd better deliver it myself.'

He stopped Fred as the boy came by. 'Do you know where Rockland School is?' he asked. 'Is it far?'

'Yes, a good way,' said Fred. 'It's my school. I go there every day. You go down there and turn to the left and . . .'

'Wait a minute, wait a minute – did you say *you* go to Rockland School?' asked the old man. 'Well, I wonder if you'd mind taking this letter with you tomorrow morning, without fail, and giving it to the headmaster?'

'Oh yes, of course,' said Fred, and he held out his hand for the note. 'I can easily do that.'

'Thanks very much,' said the man. 'Now don't forget, will you? You'll be sorry if you do!'

Fred didn't tell the old fellow what a forgettery he had! He took the note and put it into his pocket, quite meaning to give it to the headmaster the next morning.

He didn't think to himself, 'Now I *must* remember this – I will carry it home in my hand, and put it on my dressing-table so that I shall see it tomorrow morning. Then if I carry it in my hand all the way to school, I simply won't be able to help remembering to deliver it!'

No – he didn't try to remind himself at all that he had something to do for somebody else. He just put it in his pocket – and forgot ALL about it.

He didn't once think of the letter that evening. He didn't think of it the next morning. He forgot all about it when he got to school and took off his coat. There was the letter, safe in his coat pocket, hanging up in the cloakroom, and nobody knew it was there!

Friday came and went. Saturday morning came. That was the very last day of the circus! Fred asked his mother again if he could go, but she shook her head.

'I should think not, Fred! Do you know you forgot to call in and ask how poor old Mrs Jones was yesterday, and I reminded you six times at least. The poor old thing was very hurt because I didn't send to ask how she was. Certainly you can't have treats if you don't even *try* to remember something!'

Fred went out to play with his friends. They went to peep in between the railings round the field where the circus camp was. It did look so exciting. The boys wished and wished they could see it.

'The tickets are expensive,' said one boy. 'Usually they are half-price for children, but this circus has done so well, and been so crowded every night, that there have been no half-price tickets. I think the circus-owner must be jolly mean!'

Saturday went and Sunday came. That day the circus moved off. Some of the boys watched it. It was fun to see the elephants move away, dragging caravans behind them. The clowns no longer looked like clowns, for they were dressed in ordinary old jerseys and trousers. The horses were not so beautiful without their waving plumes. All the same, it was exciting to watch, as the big procession slowly made its way out of the field.

Monday morning came. All the boys went back to school again, and gathered together in the big hall for prayers and roll-call. They were about to go to their classrooms when the headmaster stood up again. He had something to say.

'One moment, boys,' he said. 'I have something to tell you. I have had a letter, this morning, from the owner of the circus that was here last week. I will read it to you.'

The boys stood still, listening. The Head began to read the letter.

'Dear Mr Kenley,

'I was astonished not to see the boys of your school at the circus on Saturday evening. I had hoped that you would allow them all to come and take the front seats, as I had offered them to you free. I hope you got the invitation safely. I gave it to one of your boys on Thursday evening to deliver to you for me as I had missed the post. He promised to do this.

'Yours faithfully,
'Phillippino.'

The headmaster folded up the letter and looked down from the platform at the

invitation from him, and forgot to deliver it. Who was it?'

Fred was frightened to say it was he who had forgotten. The boys would be so angry. He stood there, saying nothing, his face still red.

'Come, come!' said the headmaster, impatiently. 'No one is away today. It must have been one of you. It is bad enough to forget to deliver a letter, but it is a great deal worse not to be brave enough to own up to it. I've no doubt it was quite by accident that the note was not delivered to me, but please don't make matters worse by not owning up.'

Fred was terribly ashamed of himself. Was he a coward as well as a careless for-getter? Yes, he was a coward – but he'd put a stop to *that*! He would own up.

He heard his own voice, rather shaky and small.

'Please, Mr Kenley, sir, *I* got the note. I put it into my pocket, and forgot all about it. It's there still.'

surprised boys. They were nudging one another and whispering.

'We could have gone – gone for nothing!'

'We could have had the front seats! They're the best!'

'Who took the note? Why didn't he give it to the Head?'

'What a shame! The circus has gone now and we can't see it.'

One boy stood without saying a word, his face as red as a beetroot. That boy was Fred! Of course – that old man by the letter-box was Phillippino, the owner of the circus – and he had given the invita-tion to Fred – and he had forgotten all about it. It must be in his pocket still!

'I've robbed all the boys of the chance of seeing the circus for nothing!' thought Fred, with horror. 'Oh, why didn't I *try* to remember?'

'Well, boys,' said the headmaster, put-ting the letter into his pocket, 'if Mr Phillippino is right, one of you took the

There was a silence. The boys glared at Fred in anger, and then began whispering, calling the boy all kinds of hard names because he had made them miss going to the circus.

'Fetch the note,' said the Head. Fred went out and brought the letter back. The Head opened it and read it out loud.

'Dear Mr Kenley,

'It is my custom, when my circus has done well during the week, to offer on the last Saturday of the show the front seats free to any school in the district whose boys seem to me to be the best behaved. I would be glad to welcome your lads on Saturday evening, and will keep one hundred of the front seats reserved for them.

'Yours faithfully,
'Phillippino.'

'Well!' said the headmaster, folding up the note. 'I'm afraid Fred has spoilt the treat for you. Fred, will you kindly write an explanation and an apology to Mr Phillippino today. Dismiss!'

Fred had a bad time that day. Every boy was disgusted, disappointed and angry.

'Can't you remember *any*thing? You're not stupid, just lazy!'

'It's all very well to forget things that only concern yourself, but when you spoil something for other people it's different!'

'Let's leave him out of games. Who wants a boy who can't even remember to deliver a note for an old man!'

It was a tremendous shock for Fred. He must get rid of his forgettery! He must remind himself to remember things in all sorts of ways, even if it was a nuisance. He must tie knots in his handkerchief, write out notes and stick them on his dressing-table glass so that he could read them in the morning and remember. He must keep saying to himself, 'What did Mother tell me today? What did Mr Kenley ask me to do?'

'I must get back my memory and lose my forgettery,' said Fred. 'Then perhaps the boys will forget what I have done, and forgive me. It's so horrid having no friends at school.'

So he is trying hard, but it's very difficult. What's *your* memory like? I do hope it's not a forgettery like Fred's!

The Fire in the Nursery

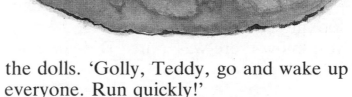

One night, after everyone had gone to bed, a hot coal rolled out of the nursery fire on to the rug. There was a lot of smoke as it burnt the rug – and then suddenly a little flame came, and the rug flared up!

The clock struck twelve – it was midnight. At once all the toys came alive and sat up.

'Fire!' shouted the teddy bear. 'Quick! Where's the toy fire engine!'

It rushed up – but there was so little water in the firemen's pails that the fire could not be put out. It ate up the rug – and then the flames went to a wooden chair and began to burn that too!

'The house will be burnt down!' wailed

the dolls. 'Golly, Teddy, go and wake up everyone. Run quickly!'

But the nursery door was tightly shut! Alas! Not one of the toys was tall enough to open it. Whatever could they do?

'It will burn the dolls' house next!' cried the clown. 'Oh my, oh my, if only we could reach the tap!'

But no one could climb up to the nursery basin – and even if they had, their tiny fingers were not strong enough to turn the big tap.

'I know, I know!' shouted the toy engine, running along the floor out of reach of the flames. 'Let us all make a great noise and perhaps we shall wake everyone up!'

'Good idea!' cried the toys. 'Teddy, you are biggest. You beat the drum!'

So Teddy beat the drum loudly – rum-ti-tum-ti-tum! And Golly got the whistle and blew it – pheeeeee! The big doll set the humming-top going – hmmmmmmm! All the clockwork toys were wound up and they jigged about for all they were worth. The sailor doll took a tin tray from the doll's house and banged that with a toy spoon. Really, you never heard such a noise!

Belinda, who was asleep in the night nursery next door, woke up with a jump. What could that noise be? She slipped out of bed and opened the nursery door – and then, how she stared and stared and stared! The toys were leaping about, shouting, beating the drum, banging the tray, the top was humming, the whistle was blowing – and oh, oh, oh! The room was on fire!

'Mummy, Daddy, quick! Fire! Fire!' shouted Belinda – and in a trice the grown-ups rushed into the nursery, and very soon there was water all over the place! It was thrown over the flames, and the fire was put out in two minutes!

'What a narrow escape!' said Mummy, looking pale. 'Belinda, darling, how did you know there was a fire? Did you smell it?'

'No, Mummy,' said Belinda. 'The toys must have known about it and wanted to wake me – because I heard such a noise, and when I got out of bed and peeped in here to see – well, you should have seen all the toys! They were as alive as could be, jumping and shouting, and . . .'

'Oh, no, Belinda, you must have dreamt that!' said Mummy – and no one would believe her.

But Belinda knows it's true – and so do the toys. As for the drum, there is a big hole in it because the bear banged it so hard that night. But nobody minds – and Belinda showed the hole to me, so I know what happened, you see!

What an Alarm!

In the village of Tickle there lived a most dishonest little pixie. His name was Light-Fingers, and it was really astonishing the amount of things he took from other people without being seen.

He would take an apple from outside Dame Cherry's shop. He would take a biscuit from the tin in Mrs Soap's store. He would pick flowers from old Dame Lucy's garden when she was out, and steal the pears from the big tree in Farmer Corn's orchard. And although everyone felt quite certain that it was Light-Fingers who was the thief, nobody ever managed to see him. He really was very clever.

'If only we could think of some way to catch him,' said Farmer Corn.

'I don't like accusing anyone of stealing unless I actually see them doing wrong with my own eyes,' said Dame Lucy.

'Quite right,' said Dame Cherry. 'We must never accuse anyone unless we can prove ourselves to be right. But dear me, how are we to prove ourselves right about naughty little Light-Fingers?'

Tick-Tock, the watch-maker, came up at that moment. He was a little bent old fellow with eyes as bright as a bird's.

'Hello, Tick-Tock,' said Farmer Corn. 'Now just you use your brains and help us. We want to catch Light-Fingers and punish him for stealing. But we don't know how to catch him, because he's so clever. Can you think of a way?'

'Yes,' said Tick-Tock, after a moment. 'I think I can. Light-Fingers comes by my shop every day on his way to and from the market. I'll put a clock on my window-sill and a notice on my door that says "GONE OUT". And if Light-Fingers doesn't take that clock I'll eat my best Sunday hat!'

'But if we hide behind a bush to watch, he's sure to know,' said Farmer Corn.

'He's so very, very smart. He wouldn't take it unless he felt quite certain he wouldn't be seen and wouldn't be found out either.'

'Now listen,' said Tick-Tock with a smile. 'That clock is going to be an *alarm*-clock – *you* know, the kind that goes off and rings a bell very loudly at a certain time. Well, I shall set the alarm for twelve o'clock, and it will go off then, just when Light-Fingers is marketing. That will give him a shock – especially when I come up and demand my clock!'

'Now that *is* a good idea!' said everyone, pleased. 'We won't be anywhere about at all when Light-Fingers takes the clock; but we'll ALL be in the market at twelve o'clock!'

So the next morning, when Light-Fingers passd by Tick-Tock's little shop, his sharp eyes saw a very fine green clock sitting by itself on the shop window-sill. Light-Fingers was surprised. Then he saw the notice on the door, 'GONE OUT', and his sharp eyes gleamed. He took a quick look round.

'There's nobody about at all,' he thought to himself. 'Not a soul! This *is* a bit of luck! And I've got my old suit on, too, with its big pockets! Hurrah! I can put the clock in nicely, and nobody will guess it is there, for I'll put my big red handkerchief over it.'

So in a trice the clock was in his pocket, with his red hanky draped over it. Then off to the market went Light-Fingers, whistling merrily. He thought he would be able to sell the clock for a lot of money when he went visiting in the next town.

The market seemed very full that morning. Light-Fingers was quite surprised. People seemed to be whispering together, and nudging one another. He wondered what it was all about. But nobody told him. Nobody whispered to him that an alarm-clock was going off at twelve o'clock that morning, and that he, Light-Fingers, was going to get a terrible shock!

At eleven o'clock the town crier went round the market, ringing his bell and shouting loudly:

'Lost or stolen! A beautiful green clock from Tick-Tock's window-sill! Lost or stolen! A beautiful green clock from Tick-Tock's window-sill! Please bring to me at once if you have it!'

'I haven't seen it!' said Dame Lucy, and she turned to Light-Fingers. 'Have *you*?'

'Dear me, no,' said naughty Light-Fingers, untruthfully. 'If I *had* seen it, I would have taken it back to poor Tick-Tock at once.'

'I'm afraid someone must have stolen it,' said Tick-Tock, sadly. 'Light-Fingers, what do you think we ought to do to the thief, if we catch him?'

'Well, if anyone was horrid enough to steal your clock, they ought to be very well punished indeed,' said Light-Fingers. 'I think the thief ought to get one hard spank from everyone in the village. If that didn't cure him, then what about taking him to the Bad-Tempered Wizard? I'm sure *he* would cure anyone in no time!'

'Good idea!' cried everyone. 'A very good idea. We agree with you, Light-Fingers.'

Now, as twelve o'clock drew nearer, everyone pressed close to Light-Fingers, eager to hear the alarm clock go off. Light-Fingers couldn't imagine why the crowds seemed to be everywhere around him. He couldn't seem to get away from them.

Then the market-clock struck twelve – and almost immediately afterwards the

94

alarm clock went off loudly. My goodness, the noise it made! It had the loudest alarm of any clock in Tick-Tock's shop, and it made Light-Fingers almost jump out of his skin!

'R-r-r-r-ring! R-r-r-ring! R-r-r-ring!'

The alarm clock went off with a terrific noise. Everyone giggled. Light-Fingers jumped high into the air and clapped his hand to his pocket. Goodness! What could be happening?

'R-r-r-r-ring! R-r-r-ring!'

'What's that ringing? Where does the noise come from?' yelled Light-Fingers.

'It comes from your pocket,' said Tick-Tock, with such a stern look on his face that Light-Fingers suddenly felt frightened. 'WHAT have you got in your pocket?'

'N-n-n-n-nothing – except my red hanky,' stammered Light-Fingers.

'Hankies don't ring like that,' said Tick-Tock.

'R-r-r-r-ring! R-r-r-ring!' went the alarm clock gaily. It seemed as if it would never stop!

'If you have nothing but your hanky in your pocket, let me see what it is that is ringing,' said Tick-Tock. 'Have you a magic ringing spell?'

'No,' said Light-Fingers. 'And, anyway, I don't want you looking into my pockets. That's a nasty thing to do.'

But before he could stop Tick-Tock, the watchmaker had put his small hand deep into Light-Finger's pocket – and pulled out – his alarm clock, still gaily ringing for all it was worth.

'HO!' said Tick-Tock, in a terrible stern voice. 'HO! So that is where my beautiful green alarm clock went – into your pocket – where many other things have gone, I've no doubt. Light-Fingers, you are a little thief, a nasty horrid little thief. I am glad you said what the punishment for a little thief should be. Let me see – what was it?'

Light-Fingers began to tremble. 'I-I-d-d-don't remember,' he stammered.

But everyone else remembered, of course. 'Light-Fingers said one hard spank from everyone in the village!' a score of voices called out gleefully. Most of the people there had had things taken from them at some time or other by Light-Fingers, so they were pleased to think they could give him one hard spank each. That would teach the bad pixie not to steal!

And so Light-Fingers got the punishment he himself suggested, and dear me, he didn't like it at all, especially when it was Farmer Corn's turn, because his hand was simply enormous and dreadfully hard.

Tick-Tock took his clock back home, and everyone giggled when they thought of the trick the clock had played on Light-Fingers.

'And remember, pixie, just remember what you said should happen to a thief who wasn't cured by spanks,' said the watch-maker solemnly. 'You said he had better be sent to the Bad-Tempered Wizard. So BE CAREFUL!'

Light-Fingers *is* careful. He has been quite honest for a long time now, so perhaps he really is cured.

The Untidy Pixie

The pixie Twinks was always in trouble. She was so dreadfully untidy! She had buttons off her shoes, hooks off her dresses, and holes in her stockings and her gloves. She had an untidy mind too – she was always leaving her things about, dropping her handkerchiefs, and losing her purse.

Now once upon a time, as she was going along the road, she met Dame Hurry-By. She was in a great hurry and she called to Twinks.

'Twinks! I want to catch the bus and I haven't time to go home and put this spell in my cupboard first. Will you take it for me?'

'Yes,' said Twinks, and she held out her hand for the tiny spell, which was like a little blue pill.

'Thank you!' said Dame Hurry-By. 'Put it on the third shelf of the cupboard, Twinks. I'll find it there when I come back!'

Twinks went on to the village to do her shopping. She had her basket with her, for she had a lot of things to buy. She had actually made out a list of things she wanted, so she felt rather pleased with herself.

She came to the shops. Now, what was on her list? She looked in the basket for it – it wasn't there. It wasn't in her hand, or in her pockets either. Bother! She must have left it at home! Twinks was cross with herself.

She did her shopping as best she could, trying to remember everything she wanted. Then she went home – and, of course, she quite forgot all about the spell that Dame Hurry-By had asked her to leave on the third shelf of her cupboard!

Well, when Dame Hurry-By got back that afternoon she went straight to the shelf in the kitchen cupboard and looked for her spell – and it wasn't there! So she

'I may have slipped the spell into one of my gloves,' said Twinks. 'I had them on this morning.'

She went to fetch her gloves. Dame Hurry-By took each one and shook it – but the spell wasn't there.

'Each of your gloves has two holes in,' she said severely. 'You should be ashamed of yourself, Twinks! The spell would certainly have fallen out of either of these. Do you think you put the spell into any of your pockets?'

'Feel,' said Twinks – so Dame Hurry-By felt – and, will you believe it, there was a hole in each of Twink's pockets! Wasn't it dreadful! Dame Hurry-By looked sterner than ever.

'Well, if you put my spell into any of these pockets it would certainly have been lost,' she said. 'You are the most untidy, careless pixie I have ever met, Twinks!'

Twinks began to cry, but Dame Hurry-By didn't look any less cross.

ran to Twink's house in a great way. 'Twinks! Twinks!' she cried. 'Where's that spell you said you would leave at my house for me?'

'Oh, my goodness!' said Twinks in dismay. 'I forgot all about it, Dame Hurry-By!'

'Well, please give it to me,' said Dame Hurry-By. 'I want it.'

Twinks stared at Dame Hurry-By and went red.

'Let me see now,' she said, 'wherever did I put it when you gave it to me?'

'In your basket, I should think,' said Dame Hurry-By. They went to look – but it wasn't there. There was a hole in the basket, and Dame Hurry-By pointed to it.

'It might have fallen out there,' she said. 'Good gracious me, Twinks, why don't you mend the basket? You'll have that hole getting bigger and then half your shopping will fall out!'

'It's no use crying,' she said. 'I feel cross because that was a very important spell. Now think hard – is there anywhere else where you might have put that spell of mine?'

'Well, I do sometimes put my handkerchief into my stocking to keep it safe when my pockets have holes in,' said Twinks. 'Maybe I put your spell into one.'

So she took off her stockings, and Dame Hurry-By looked through each one – and her frown got even bigger.

'A ladder all down the back of this stocking – and, dear me, three holes in the toe of this one,' she said. 'Do you *ever* do any mending, Twinks?'

'Not often,' said Twinks. 'Oh dear, I'm so sorry about the lost spell. Do forgive me.'

'No – I shan't forgive you,' said Dame Hurry-By. 'It cost a lot of money. You must pay me for it, Twinks.'

'But I haven't any money,' sobbed Twinks. 'I've spent it all on my shopping this morning. I've only got three pennies left in my money-box.'

'Well, what are you going to do?' asked Dame Hurry-By sternly. 'You've got to pay me for that lost spell somehow!'

'Perhaps I'd better come and do a little work for you,' said Twinks. 'I could come every day till you think I've paid for the spell.'

'Very well. Come to-morrow,' said Dame Hurry-By. 'And don't let me see you coming with any buttons off or holes in your stockings, Twinks. I won't have people looking like that in *my* house!'

So Twinks spent the rest of the day mending her clothes, and then the next morning she set off to Dame Hurry-By's house with a big apron rolled up under her arm. Dame Hurry-By set her to work. She had to wash up the breakfast things, and then do the day's washing.

Dame Hurry-By did have sharp eyes!

'Look at this cup!' she said to Twinks. 'It's so badly washed that there is still

98

some sugar left in it! And look at that plate – you haven't even washed the mustard away!'

Twinks had to do a lot of work again – and Dame Hurry-By was even more particular over the washing! She made Twinks wash some curtains three times before she said they were really clean! And when Twinks tore one she had to mend it as soon as it was ironed. My goodness – things were done at once in Dame Hurry-By's house, I can tell you!

Twinks grew very neat and clean herself. She was afraid of Dame Hurry-By's sharp eye and sharper tongue, and she looked anxiously each morning before she went to Dame Hurry-By's to see if all her buttons were on, and her dress neat, and her stockings without holes. Soon she grew quite proud of her smart look, for she was a pretty little pixie who had really spoilt herself by being so untidy.

'Do you think I've paid for that lost

spell yet?' she asked Dame Hurry-By one morning.

'Yes,' said Dame Hurry-By. 'And I'm going to give you a silver shilling for yourself, because you have got so much better lately. Here it is – put it into your purse and DON'T lose it, Twinks!'

Twinks got out her little purse and opened it – and whatever do you suppose she saw inside? Guess!

Yes – the lost spell! The little pixie had put it there to be safe, when Dame Hurry-By had given it to her a week or two back. It was the only place she hadn't thought of looking in! Silly Twinks!

'Oh, look, Dame Hurry-By!' said Twinks. 'Here's the spell after all! I had it all the time, quite safely! Oh, how foolish I am!'

'Well, you may still be foolish but you are no longer careless and untidy!' said Dame Hurry-By, with a laugh. 'Here is your silver shilling. Run off home now, and don't forget all the things you've learnt from me!'

Twinks hasn't forgotten them yet – you should see her mending her stockings each week, and sewing on buttons! It was a good thing she thought she had lost the spell, wasn't it!

Linda's Little House

On her birthday Linda had an exciting present. She undid the paper, and unwrapped a box. On the front of the box was a picture of a pretty little house, with a green roof, some windows, a green front door, and two red chimneys.

'Oh!' said Linda. 'What a darling house!'

She took off the box-lid – and there, inside, were red bricks, green tiles for the roof, little glass windows, a small green front door and two red chimneys.

'You see, it's for you to build,' said Mummy. 'If you look well at the picture, and copy it, you will see exactly how to build that pretty little house.'

So after breakfast Linda sat down on the floor and began to build the new little house.

She built the walls. She slipped the windows into the spaces she had left in the walls. She put on the green-tiled roof very carefully. She slid the chimneys into the holes left for them. And last of all she put in the little front door, which could be hung on a small hinge and opened and shut properly. It even had a tiny knocker on it, which made the smallest rat-tat-tat you ever heard.

'Look, Mummy!' said Linda. 'Isn't it lovely? Now I know how to build a house! Would you like to see me do it all over again?'

'Yes, I would,' said Mummy. So Linda knocked the tiny house down, and began to build it all over again. She knocked it down and built it six times that day. The toys watched her every time, and thought she was very clever.

That night she left the little house standing by the toy cupboard when she went to bed. The golliwog opened the door, bent himself down low and walked in. The teddy bear was too fat to get inside. The clockwork mouse ran in, and the small dolls from the dolls' house. They all thought it was the nicest house they had ever seen.

'Isn't Linda clever to build it up like that,' said the golly. 'She's so quick too. Really, it doesn't take her ten minutes to do it!'

Linda often played with the little house. Then someone gave her a paint-box and she forgot about the house for a time, and painted pictures instead.

Now one night, when the toys were playing in the nursery, there came a knocking at the window.

'That's Dance-About the pixie!' cried the bear and ran to open the window. It *was* Dance-About – but a very sad pixie she was. She cried so many tears on the window-sill that it looked as if it had been raining there.

'Whatever's the matter?' asked the bear.

'Oh, toys – you know my dear little house in the woods?' said Dance-About. 'The one made out of that big toadstool? Well, it's gone. A horrid boy came along this afternoon and kicked it to bits. It's a good thing I wasn't there, or I'd have been kicked to bits too. Now I've got no house at all. There aren't any more toadstools growing. It's cold without a house – so I've come to ask you what I ought to do.'

The golliwog looked round at the little house Linda so often built. It was standing by the toy cupboard. 'What about Linda's house?' he said. 'I shouldn't think it would matter if you had that. It is a lovely little house, just big enough for you, Dance-About.'

'So it is,' said the pixie, dancing in at the front door, and out again. 'But how can I take the house to the woods?'

'It knocks down, and it's quite easy to build up again,' said the bear. 'Look – this is how you knock it down.'

He knocked it all down. Then the toys neatly put the bricks, the chimneys and everything into the box, and popped on the lid. The golly and the bear between them carried the box to the woods, and Dance-About showed them where she wanted the house built.

But it wasn't so easy to build as the bear had thought. It was true he had often watched Linda building it, but that wasn't the same as building it himself. He put the chimney where the window ought to be and didn't leave any room for the door. It was a dreadful muddle.

'We'd better go and ask Linda to come and help,' said the golliwog at last. 'Oh, dear – I hope she won't mind us borrowing the house like this. Bear, go and fetch her, will you?'

So, much to her surprise, Linda was awakened by the bear, who told her what they wanted. She got out of bed at once, excited.

'It was rather naughty of you, bear, to carry my house off like that without even asking me,' she said, as she put on her dressing-gown and slippers. 'Of course, I'll come – and I'll build the house and let Dance-About have it. Fancy seeing a pixie in the middle of the night like this!'

The bear took her to the place in the woods where the pixie was. All the other toys were there, too, standing round the heap of bricks and tiles on the grass.

Linda began to build the house. The moon shone down and gave her enough light to see by. In ten minutes the house was finished. There it stood in the moonlight, with its red chimneys, shining windows and little front door. It looked so real.

'Oh, thank you!' said Dance-About, skipping in at the door. 'It's beautiful. Just the right size, too. I'll get some curtains for the windows tomorrow, and buy some furniture. And I'll give a tea-party when the house is ready to live in. You'll come, won't you, Linda?'

'Of course!' said Linda, joyfully, and off she went back to bed. She could hardly believe it was all true next day when she woke up! But the box was gone, and she was almost sure the bear gave her a smile when she looked at him.

And today she found a note tucked under the bear's fat arm. It says:

'Dear Linda,

My tea-party is at four o'clock today. Do come. Tippy-Toppy Tarts with cream, and Squishy Buns with honey.
'Love from Dance-About.'

Linda's going, of course, and she's going to tell me what the Tippy-Toppy Tarts are, and the Squishy Buns. I hope she brings a few back with her, don't you!

To Linda

Dear Linda
My tea-party is at four-o'clock today.
Do come. Tippy-Toppy Tarts with cream and Squishy Buns with honey.
Love from Dance-About

The Rude Little Rabbit

There was once a little speckled rabbit called Bobtail who was very rude. He called cheeky names out after anyone he met, and he always answered back when anyone scolded him.

'Hallo, pins and needles!' he would say to Prickles the hedgehog. Prickles always got very much annoyed when anyone called him that.

'I shall tell your mother,' Prickles said.

'Tell my father and my mother, my brothers and my sisters, my grandmothers and my grandfathers, my great-grandmothers and my great-grandfathers!' Bobtail said.

'I suppose you think you're clever,' said Prickles.

'I don't think it, I know it!' sang out Bobtail.

Then he saw the beautiful kingfisher fly down to the river bank. The blue and green bird was dazzling to look at, but he hadn't much of a tail, which always made him feel a bit sad.

'Left your tail at home this morning?' asked Bobtail, popping his head out of a bush.

'If you were my child I'd spank you and put you to bed,' said the kingfisher, annoyed.

'If I were your child I'd find you a new tail and stitch it on!' said Bobtail rudely.

But one day he was rude to the wrong person! He was rude to the Spotted Goblin, who lived in the hollow oak tree.

The Spotted Goblin had once dropped a pot of red paint, and it had splashed up

and spotted him with red all over. As it was magic paint, he hadn't been able to wash it off, so he had to have the spots for always.

Bobtail saw him coming along, and he pulled his whiskers and thought of a joke. He knew that measles had spots, so he called out after the Goblin:

'Hallo, Measles! How are your spots?'

The Goblin turned round and glared. 'If you dare to say that again I'll put a spell on your ears!' he said.

Bobtail didn't believe him. 'Hallo, Measles, how are your spots?' he said again, and then rushed off to his hole at once.

'Kikky, rooni, billinoona!' shouted the Goblin in an angry voice. It was a spell for rabbits' ears, but Bobtail didn't know it.

The spell worked. When Bobtail got to his hole and tried to flatten his ears down over his head, as all rabbits must do when they run under ground, Bobtail found that he couldn't put his ears down at all! No, they just stayed upright. It was queer.

He tried to force his way into the hole. His mother saw him, and spoke to him sharply. 'You've left your ears up. Put them down, silly child.'

'I can't,' said Bobtail, in dismay.

'Don't be stupid!' said his mother. 'All rabbits can put their ears down.'

But Bobtail couldn't. It wasn't a bit of good. His ears stayed straight up, and even when his mother tried to bend them down she couldn't. She only made Bobtail cry out with pain.

'Well, you can't come into the burrow unless you put your ears down,' said his mother. 'You'll wear them out. What have you been doing to get your ears like this?'

'I was rude to the Spotted Goblin,' said Bobtail, looking ashamed. 'I said: "Hallo, Measles, how are your spots?" '

'What! You were as rude as that!' cried his mother. 'I'm ashamed of you. You deserve to have a spell put into your ears, you really do.'

Well poor Bobtail had a bad time after that. You see, he couldn't dash into his hole with all the other rabbits when an enemy came along. Sometimes it was a sly fox, coming to get a young rabbit for dinner. Sometimes it was a dog hunting. Other times it was a farmer with a gun.

Bobtail dashed off into the bushes, but it was easy for foxes or dogs to smell him out. He ran and ran, and they ran after him. He only managed to escape by leaping into a hollow tree and staying there quite still whilst his enemies rushed past.

'This is dreadful,' thought poor Bobtail. 'What a life I shall lead with ears like this. I never knew before how important it is for a rabbit's ears to be able to flop over.'

One day he saw the Spotted Goblin standing at the top of Steep Hill. Bobtail made his way humbly to him.

'Please, Spotted Goblin,' he said. 'I'm very sorry I was rude to you. Take the spell out of my ears. I'll never be rude to anyone again.'

'I can't take the spell out,' said the Goblin. 'There's only one way of curing those long ears of yours – and that is to throw you from the top of the hill to the bottom!'

'Oh no, oh no!' cried Bobtail, wishing he had never gone near the Goblin. But the Spotted Goblin lunged out with his foot and gave Bobtail a hard kick.

He rolled down the hill, over and over, over and over, head and back and heels and ears and tail, over and over. His ears were bent and he squealed in pain. He lost two whiskers. He hurt his foot. He bruised his bobtail – and he certainly bent his ears back till they nearly broke!

He sat up, feeling very shaky, at the bottom of the hill. He felt himself all over to see if he was still there. Two young rabbits came out to look at him.

'Do you usually come down the hill like that?' they said.

'Now don't you be cheeky!' said Bobtail, and he turned to chase them. They went

down their hole – and he followed them. Half-way down he stopped in delight.

'My ears are all right again! They bent themselves down when I went into the hole. Oh good – now they are cured!'

But it was a very painful cure, for Bobtail was so stiff and bruised for days after that he could hardly lollop in and out of his hole.

'I hope you're cured of your rudeness now,' his mother said to him.

'Mother, I'm the very politest rabbit that ever was,' said Bobtail.

'What a change!' said his mother. And it certainly was!

Pippitty's Joke

Pippitty was a pixie – but what a naughty one. The things he did! He stuck a stamp on the pavement, and watched every one trying in vain to pick it up! He put a parcel in the gutter, and when the passers-by bent to see what it was it suddenly jerked away and made them jump – for Pippitty had got a black thread tied to it, and he was holding the other end round the corner.

When he got caught by Mother Go-Along, she spanked him so hard that he cried a whole bucket of tears.

'I'll pay you out for this spanking!' said Pippitty, and he ran off home. When he got there he wondered and he wondered how he could play a trick on Mother Go-Along without her knowing that it was he who was doing it.

And at last he thought of a joke. 'I'll fly up to her roof – and take a can of water with me – and sit by her chimney – and pour water down it on to her fire! Then it will sizzle and smoke and she'll think some one has put a spell on it and will be so frightened!' chuckled naughty Pippitty to himself. Wasn't he a monkey?

Well, he waited till night came. Then up to the chimney he flew, carrying with him a big can of water. He knew which was the kitchen chimney, for smoke was coming from it. My word, Mother Go-Along must be having a good fire, for the smoke was simply pouring out!

Pippitty grinned to himself. He sat on the edge of the chimney and tipped up the heavy can of water. Splishy-splashy-splishy-splashy – it hurried down that sooty chimney to the fire below!

Mother Go-Along was sitting in her rocking-chair by the fire, knitting peacefully. Suddenly, as a trickle of water reached the flames, the fire gave a loud sizzle-sizzle, sizzle, and sent out a cloud of black smoke!

'Good gracious!' said Mother Go-Along, in alarm, 'What's all this?'

She poked the fire – it burnt up again

after a while, so Mother Go-Along sat down once more to her knitting. Flames shot up the chimney.

It was nice and warm.

Pippitty, sitting up on the roof, thought it was time to send down another lot of water – so he tipped up the can. An extra big lot went down – splishy-splashy-splishy-splashy! It reached the fire.

'SIZZLE-SOZZLE-SIZZLE-SOZZLE!' What a noise the fire made when the water tried to put it out! Mother Go-Along jumped up in fright. Clouds of dark smoke billowed out into her kitchen.

'It's a spell someone has put on my fire!' she cried. 'Yes – a spell!'

She cried this out in such a loud voice that Pippitty heard it, up on the roof. He grinned and chuckled and nearly fell off the chimney in delight. Aha! This was a fine punishment for Mother Go-Along! That would teach her to spank him! Oho!

He tipped up the can and sent down another lot of water – but this was too much for poor Mother Go-Along. When the fire said, 'Sizzle-sozzle,' again she ran out of the door squealing. 'Help! Help! There's a spell on my fire!' she cried.

Pippitty laughed so much that he fell right off the chimney and nearly slid down the roof. He decided to wait and see what would happen. Presently Mother Go-Along came back with Dame Quick-Eyes. Pippitty could hear them talking.

'I tell you there's a dreadful spell on my fire!' said Mother Go-Along. 'It keeps shouting, "Sizzle-Sozzle" at me, and sending out clouds of black smoke.'

'Dear, dear,' said Dame Quick-Eyes. 'Well, we must see what we can do about it!'

They went indoors. Pippitty put his ear to the chimney to hear what they said. He still had a little water left in his can. What fun to give old Dame Quick-Eyes a fright too.

The fire was out. Dame Quick-Eyes told Mother Go-Along to make another. So in

a few minutes sticks were burning merrily, and a nice fire roared up the chimney. The two dames sat down to see if the spell would work again.

They didn't have to wait long! Pippitty tipped up his can – splishy-sploshy-splishy-sploshy – down went the water, rushing through the chimney to the fire.

'Sizzle-sozzle-sizzle-sozzle!' shouted the fire and a cloud of smoke blew out! Dame Quick-Eyes had quick ears as well as quick eyes, and she had heard the splashing sound of the water – and she had seen, too, the wetness that came around the hearth before the heat dried it up. *Some-*

one, yes, *some*one was pouring water down Mother Go-Along's chimney! Ho ho! So that was it!

Dame Quick-Eyes whispered to Mother Go-Along. 'I'll catch the one who's doing this! Have you got a butterfly-net or a fishing-net anywhere about?'

'I've got an old fishing-net in the cupboard,' whispered back Mother Go-Along. 'I'll get it. Whatever are you going to do?'

She fetched the net. Pippitty, who had his ear to the chimney, couldn't hear a word. He was longing to know if he had frightened Dame Quick-Eyes too!

Dame Quick-Eyes was busy – very busy! She had stolen to the door and opened it. She had rubbed a spell on the fishing-net to make it bigger – and bigger – and bigger! It grew so long that it was higher than the roof! And then Dame Quick-Eyes looked up to the chimney – and, very faintly indeed against the cloudy night sky she spied someone sitting on the chimney! Aha!

She held up her long, long net – she held it just over the chimney – she brought it down on the chimney – smack! And she caught Pippitty!

What a surprise he got when that net came down on him! He jumped so much that he almost fell down the chimney himself! He couldn't get out of the net, however much he struggled.

Dame Quick-Eyes twisted the net round, with Pippitty inside, and brought it down to the ground. She made the net smaller in a trice, put out her hand and grabbed Pippitty.

'So it's you, is it, you monkey!' she said. 'I might have guessed it!' She took the frightened pixie in to Mother Go-Along, who stared in surprise.

'Pippitty sat up on the roof and poured water down your chimney,' said Dame Quick-Eyes. 'That was what made the fire say "Sizzle-sozzle," and made the black smoke too. Do you want to spank him again, Mother Go-Along?'

'Oh no, don't spank me!' begged Pippitty. 'Anything else but that!'

'Spanking's no good for a naughty pixie like that,' said Mother Go-Along. 'I've tried it once – and see what happened. He just came and poured water down my chimney. No, Dame Quick-Eyes, I shall do something better than that. You said he was a monkey, so he shall be! When he's tired of being a real one, I'll turn him back into a pixie again and see if he can behave himself!'

She muttered three magic words over Pippitty – and in a trice he turned into a little brown monkey with big brown eyes and a long tail. What a shock for him that was!

He scurried away out of the cottage to hide himself. What *would* his friends say when they saw him? Oh dear, oh dear!

'He behaved like a little monkey, and now that he is one he ought to be pleased,' said Dame Quick-Eyes.

But he wasn't! The funny thing is that now he *is* a monkey he doesn't behave like one – he behaves like a perfectly good pixie! I expect Mother Go-Along will change him back to his own shape soon – but if you happen to see a small monkey anywhere about with soft brown eyes, have a good look at him. It may be that rascal of a Pippitty!

Sally's Stitch

Sally was a little girl who was always laughing, so you can guess she was rather nice. I do like people who laugh, don't you? Well, you would have liked Sally very much. Everybody did.

One day she went for a walk across the fields. She went quietly, for the grass was thick and soft. And quite suddenly she came across five or six pixies playing the most surprising games. Sally knew they were pixies because she had seen pictures of them in books, just as you have. She was simply delighted. She sat down behind a bush and watched.

'I can stand on my head on the gate-post!' cried a small pixie – and he did. It was really funny to see him.

'I can curl myself up into a ball and roll along!' cried another. And he curled him-self up, arms and legs and all, and began to roll over and over just like a ball. All the pixies laughed to see him.

'Can you bounce yourself, can you bounce yourself?' squealed a pixie nearby. 'Oh, do try!'

'Of course I can!' cried the ball-pixie, and he threw himself up into the air. 'Look out – I'm going to bounce!'

And he bounced. Goodness, how he bounced! Just as if he were a big rubber ball. Up into the air he went, and down he came again. He bounced on to a prickly thistle, gave a loud yell, and bounced high again.

Sally began to laugh. She couldn't help it. She laughed till the tears came into her eyes. Then she got a stitch in her side from laughing, and that made her feel very uncomfortable. 'Oh dear,' she said, 'oh dear!' And she put her hand against her side to try and ease the stitch there. You know how funny you feel when you get a stitch in your side from running or laughing, don't you?

The pixies heard Sally's laughter. It was a nice sound. They ran round the bush to see who was there. And they found Sally, laughing away, with her hand pressed to her side.

'What's the matter?' they cried anxiously. 'Why do you hold yourself there? Are you hurt?'

'Oh, I've got such a big stitch in my side!' said Sally. 'I can't get rid of it. Oh, it hurts me! I can't breathe properly. I can't walk with it, either.'

'Poor little girl!' cried a big pixie. 'Who put the stitch there? Did you sew it there yourself? Was the needle sharp?'

'Of course not,' said Sally, beginning to giggle again. 'Don't be so silly.'

'Poor child!' said the pixies, looking at Sally out of their funny green eyes. 'She's got a stitch in her side. Somebody has stitched her up so that she can't walk properly. Poor child.'

'Oh, don't make me laugh again or my stitch will get worse!' cried Sally. 'Oh dear – it's the worst stitch I've ever had. But really, you did look so funny when you

bounced on that thistle, pixie. Oh my – I shall start laughing again if I'm not careful!'

She tried to walk a few steps, but she couldn't because of the stitch in her side. The pixies felt really sorry for her. They talked among themselves.

'Let's call Dame Snippit. She can take out the stitch. The poor girl will never get home. What a shame that somebody has stitched her up like that.'

'Dame Snippit! Dame Snippit!' called a pixie, loudly. 'Are you anywhere about? You're wanted.'

To Sally's enormous surprise, a neat little door opened in a nearby oak tree and out stepped a funny, plump old dame, with her hair in ringlets, and her waist all hung about with scissors and tape-measures.

'What's the matter?' she asked.

'This poor child has got a stitch in her side, so she can't walk,' explained a pixie. 'Can you take out the stitch?'

'I could snip it,' said Dame Snippit, taking up her largest pair of scissors. 'That's the quickest way of taking out a stitch, you know.'

'Oh, I don't want it snipped,' said Sally, in alarm. 'It's not that kind of stitch, really it isn't.'

'Well, what sort of a stitch is it then, my dear?' asked Dame Snippit, in surprise.

'Well – it's a laughing-stitch,' said Sally.

'Never heard of one,' said Dame Snippit. 'Come, come – let me snip it for you, then you can walk. You shouldn't let people put a stitch in your side like that. Very silly of you.'

'I didn't, I didn't,' said Sally, and she tried to run away. But the stitch in her side caught her and she had to stop. She saw Dame Snippit take up her scissors again.

Then Sally remembered that her mother had always said she could get rid of a stitch in her side by bending over and touching her toes with her fingers.

'I'd better try that before Dame Snippit

does anything stupid!' thought the little girl. So she bent herself right over and touched her toes. When she stood up straight again, lo and behold! her stitch was quite gone! Hurray!

'The stitch is gone!' she cried. 'It's all right, pixie, it's all right, Dame Snippit. The stitch is gone.'

'I suppose you broke it when you bent over,' said Dame Snippit, in astonishment. 'Well, well – don't you go having stitches inside you any more. Most uncomfortable, I call it.'

Sally said goodbye and ran home. On the way she remembered again how the pixie had bounced himself on the prickly thistle, and she stopped and began to laugh.

And she got another stitch in her side! But she didn't say a word about it. No – she wasn't going to have Dame Snippit trying to snip the stitch with her big scissors!

Do you ever get a stitch? Well, try Sally's way of curing it, and see if it goes!

Here Comes Captain Bang!

Yes – it *was* Captain Bang and all his soldiers! Everyone stared at the horsemen on the far-away hillside – and a loud sound came to their ears. What was it?

It was the noise of horses' hooves as they galloped along. Clippitty-clop, gallop-a-gallop, clippity-clop, gallop-a-gallop!

'On, soldiers, on, faster, faster!' roared Captain Bang. 'There's the circus yonder – that's the one that Bom has joined!'

'We'll catch him, we'll catch him,' shouted back the soldiers, and faster and faster they went.

Captain Bang had heard that very morning that Bom had been seen at Mr Toots' Circus, and now he meant to get hold of him, take him prisoner, and lock him up in the fort once more. Do look out, Bom – they will soon be at the circus!

Captain Bang waved his sword as he galloped on, looking very fierce. He slowed down as he came to the circus field, and his men jogged along to the gate – what a lot of them there were!

Mr Toots didn't know that they were after little Bom and he stared at them in wonder. 'Whatever do they want?' he thought. 'Good gracious – they are riding in at the circus-gate, the captain at their head. How fierce he looks!'

Bom watched them come in at the gate too, and he felt very frightened. 'Whatever can I do?' he thought. 'I'm no match for Captain Bang and his men!'

He sat down on his drum because his legs were shaking so much that they wouldn't hold him. 'Now let me think hard,' said Bom, and put his head in his hands. He thought and he thought.

'I haven't time to run away. And what's the good of hiding? They will search the

'I won't let them capture you!' said Mr Long-Legs. 'I'll hide you, little Bom.'

'But where can *you* hide me?' said Bom, surprised.

'Now listen,' said Mr Long-Legs, sitting down beside Bom. 'Listen carefully, Bom. Go and get my stilts, and my long, long trousers! You've just got time to put them on while Captain Bang is talking to Mr Toots. Go behind that tent – go on, now! Captain Bang will never guess it is you when you look so very, very tall!'

'Oh – what a fine idea!' said Bom, and jumped up. He fetched the stilts and the long, long trousers and ran behind the big tent.

'Now to put them on,' he said and drew the long trousers over his short legs, ruckling them up – and then he strapped the stilts on and stood up with Mr Long-Legs' help. The trousers fell over the tall stilts and covered them right down to the ground – and how tall Bom looked then!

Mr Long-Legs laughed. 'People will

whole circus for me. Oh dear, oh dear – I shall *have* to go back to that horrid little cell and be locked up in the fort!'

Someone came by at that moment. It was Mr Long-Legs the stilt-walker – but he wasn't wearing his stilts just then, he looked an ordinary little fellow as small as Bom. He stared at the little drummer sitting on his drum and was surprised to see him so sad.

'Hey, Bom! What's wrong?' he called. 'And my goodness me – look at all those soldiers in our field! What have *they* come for?'

Bom nodded his head sadly. 'Yes – I see them. And oh, Long-Legs, they've come for *me*. They'll capture me and take me back to prison in the fort.'

'Well, run away, then – quickly!' cried Mr Long-Legs. 'Hurry, Bom!'

'There's no time to run away,' said Bom. 'They've all got horses – they would soon overtake me. Oh, Long-legs, whatever can I do?'

think you are me!' he said. 'Now, start walking, Bom – and don't go near that loud-voiced captain!'

Bom, still feeling very scared, walked off on the long stilts, looking enormously tall. Away he went over the field, keeping as far from the soldiers as he could.

Captain Bang was being very rude to Mr Toots. 'Hey, you! Bring out Bom, the little drummer, or I will tell my men to capture you and clap you into prison too!' he shouted.

'Don't talk to me like that,' said Mr Toots, angrily. 'How do you know if Bom is here or not?'

'Well, look – that's his drum over there!' bellowed Captain Bang. And sure enough, there was Bom's drum nearby, with the two drumsticks laid neatly on top of it. What a pity!

'He must be here, or he would have taken his drum. Fetch him out, Mr Toots, fetch him out!' Captain Bang shouted so loudly that even Mr Toots felt scared.

One by one the circus folk came up to listen. Madame Wooky and her five monkeys came, and Jumbo and his keeper, the four clowns, and all the rest. How they disliked Captain Bang and his loud voice! They looked at him, but nobody said a word. They all hoped that little Bom was safely hidden away somewhere!

'Soldiers! Search the camp!' cried Captain Bang, and off they all went. They looked in every tent. They peered into the caravans. One soldier even opened the bear's cage – and what a shock he had when he walked inside!

The bears were fast asleep but they all woke up when he came in hunting for little Bom! They began to grunt angrily and he was in such a fright that he rushed out and left the cage-door open!

'The bears' cage is open!' shouted Smiler the clown. 'Look out – the bears will come lumbering out into the field.' Someone scampered quickly over the grass to the cage.

Who was it? – why, Trip the little monkey! He knew how to open and shut the doors, and SLAM! He shut the cage-door and fastened it. Clever Trip! All the bears were growling and grunting because they did not like Captain Bang's loud voice.

Mr Long-Legs did not like Captain Bang either. 'I'll go and whisper something in Jumbo's big ear!' he thought, and he ran to the elephant and whispered to him. Jumbo nodded his head and flapped his ears and smiled. Aha! Old Jumbo will soon be up to mischief. Look out, Captain Bang!

Jumbo walked over to a trough of water that the horses drank from. He put his trunk into the water and drew up a great deal – but he didn't drink it!

He ran over to Captain Bang and squirted the water all over him. What a shock for him! 'It's pouring with rain!' shouted the captain. 'Where's my umbrella?'

Everyone laughed loudly, and Long-Legs patted Jumbo and whispered to him

again. 'I'll buy you twelve new currant buns for doing that!' he said.

Captain Bang was very angry. 'How dare your elephant do that!' he said to Mr Toots. 'You just wait till I find Bom. I'll take him prisoner at once – and that elephant too!'

And then suddenly the captain saw Bom in the long, long trousers, towering high above him – but he couldn't see the stilts, of course, inside the trousers. He stared up at Bom in surprise and fright, his eyes running all the way up the long trousers, past the coat, right to Bom's little head at the top, with his hat looking as if it almost touched the sky!

And then Mr Long-Legs, who was standing just beside the captain, began to sing loudly:

116

Here comes Bom,
The Big Big Bom.
He's grown so high
He bumps the sky.
His shoes he can't see
For he's tall as can be.
Here comes Bom,
The BIG – BIG – BOM!

Bom walked on his stilts over to the astonished Captain Bang and towered right above him. He shouted down in a very loud voice: 'WHAT DO YOU WANT WITH ME, LITTLE CAPTAIN BANG? SHALL I KNOCK OFF YOUR HAT? SHALL I PICK UP YOUR HORSE?'

'No, no, no!' cried Captain Bang in fright, and he galloped away. 'Follow me, men! We can't fight a giant! Bring that drum with you!'

One of the soldiers bent down from his horse and picked up the drum and sticks – but Jumbo the elephant put out his great trunk and snatched the drum away from him. The soldier gave a frightened shout and rode off. He hadn't got the drum – but he held on to the drumsticks! Then away went all the soldiers at top speed, gallop-a-gallop-a-gallop!

Bom looked down from the top of the stilts and was very upset when he saw that one of the soldiers had his drumsticks. He couldn't go after him because he could only walk slowly on the stilts.

But *somebody* went after the soldiers for him! It was Trip, the clever little monkey. He leapt through the trees by the roadside, and dropped neatly down on to the soldier with the drum-sticks! He snatched them away and leapt off into the trees again. What a surprise for the soldier! He almost fell of his horse in fright.

Trip went back to the circus field and climbed all the way up the very tall Bom to give him the drumsticks. Then he sat on Bom's shoulder, very proud indeed. Bom soon took off the stilts and was his own

small self again. 'Thank you, Mr Long-Legs, for your stilts,' he said. 'And thank you, Jumbo, for your help, and you too, Trip, for yours. Here's another toffee for you, little monkey.'

'Stay with us and join our circus,' said Mr Toots. 'We like you very much, Bom.'

'No, Mr Toots. I can't stay,' said Bom. 'I'm off on my adventures again. I'm going to see the world! Good-bye, everybody!'

'Good-bye!' called everyone, and Jumbo put his trunk round Bom's neck, and Trip the monkey hugged him too. Then the clowns led the way to the gate, turning head-over-heels.

And away went Bom the little drummer to seek another adventure, beating his big drum and marching valiantly as he sang his little song:

Bom-diddy-bom,
Here I come, come, come,
Bom-diddy-bom,
With my drum, drum, drum,
Bom-diddy-bom-diddy-bom-bom-bom . . .

Good-bye, Bom! See you soon again!

118